The Mountain of Light

The Mountain of Light

Jim Crumley

Whittles Publishing

Published by
Whittles Publishing Limited,
Roseleigh House,
Latheronwheel,
Caithness, KW5 6DW,
Scotland, UK
www.whittlespublishing.com

Typeset by
Samantha Barden

ISBN 1-904445-04-7

Printed by
J.W. Arrowsmith Ltd., Bristol

*To the Sons and Daughters of the Rock
Including My Own*

CONTENTS

cɔɑ

CHAPTER 1

ACROSS THE BRIDGE OF LANDSCAPES

ഽൟൟ

THE WANDERER'S winter on the Rock was done. He was leaving, returning to the mountains that had offered him up and held him in check all winter, a tethered wolf.

One morning of early spring, a small gathering watched him go, a bunched fist of five men on a knoll below the castle 'that's the dark crouching angel on the shoulder of all of us', as Rab would have it. The five had been six before the Wanderer came (there had also been a woman – Bella) and for that winter, with the Wanderer in their company, they had been seven. But he was away that early spring morning and Bella was with him. The two figures were already beyond the old Stirling Bridge and barely visible. 'That bridge of landcapes,' he had once called it, and he held it just as dear as the townsfolk did but for utterly different reasons. To the natives it was the bridge where Wallace beat the English, and no matter that it was a replacement bridge for the wooden one where history was made, it was still history enough, and a tangible symbolic link with their own past, with that Stirling and that Scotland that was. To the Wanderer, though, crossing the bridge brought rest and let light into the darkness he had borne as a burden.

Rab muttered into his beard:

'We'll never forget you, Neebor, you and your stories and your poems.'

Stories?

He knew better than that. That's the way it was for a few burdened folk.

The Wanderer and Bella had paused on the crown of the bridge, waved and turned again for the mountains twenty miles off, then north, then God knows where after that. Not that the Wanderer did much beseeching to the kind of Scottish God they preached hereabouts. By dusk the pair of them would be back among the mountains again. That was what they wanted, the Poet-Wanderer and his Bella.

Then Sammy, the restless thinker of the group, came quietly to Rab's shoulder as the pair of them waved, and said:

'Rab…'

'Aye?'

'I've been thinking.'

'Aye?' (Sammy usually had been.)

'Aye.'

'And…?'

'Do you think he was *sent* to…you know…to *get* her?'

'Sent?'

'Aye, sent, like the laddie in his story, if it wiz a story. Mind the stuff aboo' the south wind claiming a new swan?'

'Mm. I mind. Or maybe reclaiming an old yin, Sammy.'

'Eh?!'

Sammy's thinking had not considered that possibility. Rab put a hand on his friend's shoulder.

'Know your trouble, Sammy? Your trouble is you aye think too much. No just that. Yur too good at it.'

'Eh?'

'Later, Sammy, eh? Some other time.'

Rab stifled Sammy's frustration with silence. Sammy knew the signs, knew better than to try and breach that cordon of wordlessness. He could do that, Rab, put himself out of reach while he stood next to you. If you didn't know him so well you'd call it rude, but either way, it set him apart from the others. So Sammy thought about that instead.

He thought what he might have said this time that had trespassed on the inner sanctum where Rab fended off trespassers with an unsuffering silence. He re-ran the conversation in his own mind. He worried at the daftness of the notion he'd given voice to, yet as soon as he rebuked himself he recognised how the notion had troubled Rab, in which case, *was* it nonsense? And now, as if that wasn't enough, he had silence to trouble him.

He would have to wait for Rab's 'some other time', if there was a 'some other time' at all. You could never tell with Rab. Sammy dared a fast sideways-and-upwards glance and saw a black, thundercloud brow, and wondered at the strifes warring there.

Stirling was 'Strivelyn' in the old tongue – the Place of Strifes. The five men walked silently back, up through the

Top of the Town, that stony grey warren of old houses that traipses up towards the castle. A thronged and decrepit town it was then, weary as the Rock itself, weary for all those old eras of strifes on behalf of that old Scotland whose glories it had once accommodated.

Yet amid the weariness, a stoical tribe still lived and loved and fought among themselves and laboured and died, for were they not hewn from the Rock itself in the beginning? Had they not inherited for a birthright the stoicism of the Rock that had in its time turned aside the Great Ice, even the invading sea, let alone the English? Who knew, folk said, when the Rock might come into its own again, lead that old Scotland again through new eras of strifes to new glories? They said it quietly and they couched the idea unpompously, but they said it, and some of them believed it. They were fragments of their own country's posterity and they knew it, descendants of the history makers, caretakers of history's stage. There was no reason to believe it was all done. Just a lull between strifes.

The five trudged on up past the last house, the ragged rhythm of boot tackits sclaffing a flinty spark here and there among stone setts, five gray men looking at their feet, bowed by thought and thoughtlessness, quite untouched by the spring in the morning's step. They turned in at the back bar of the Castle Inn, an ancient howff that had been the forge of their extraordinary winter. They were Rab and Sammy, Walter, Chas and Robert, and they were a brotherhood, unexplained and unarticulated and unquestioned, but closer than just friends, as interdependent as St Kildans in their single oceanic street.

The bar had just opened (why else would they be this high on the Rock?), disinfected with the morning-after's chlorinated hangover, and empty. The fire was on (when was it not?) and its coaly essence was already subduing the sharp edge of the chlorine, blunting it to something more familiar, reliable, dirty, wholesome. They took drinks to the fire, their silence unbroken. For twenty minutes it knotted tongues and chafed throats. It lay on the room like a snow cloud on Ben Ledi, a snuffing hood. It heaped drifts on the five of them so that such thoughts as they achieved would flounder and lose their way. It seemed to them now that he had moved that old town on its Rock about ten miles nearer the mountains, that Wanderer. When they looked west to north along their familiar mountain skyline, they saw with unfamiliar eyes, as though every perspective was new.

Robert gatecrashed the silence at last. Nature's abhorrence of a vacuum was a paltry force beside Robert's distrust of silence. He didn't agree with silence, especially one as unnatural as this one had become. It was not much of a speech, but at least it was speech.

'Shhhhhhhit,' he said softly, spinning out the 'sh' to mitigate the force of the curse and camouflage his helplessness, an uncanny respect for the silence considering it was Robert.

They all looked up at that, grateful for talk, eager for more, but Robert was mostly more a source of sound than conversation. All he had broken was the silence, not the unease. So he said it again, shorter and sharper this time, like a well-aimed spit. They met each other's eyes then, any one face as familiar as anything any of them would see in a mirror. There were half-smiles, as close as that coterie ever came to self-consciousness. They grunted monosyllables down onto the long table as they might once have thrown down cards, spades when they wanted diamonds.

Aye, once. It was a while since they'd played cards. He'd changed all that, had them telling stories – and poems. *Poems! Here!*

Chas refocused on his glass and realised he could see the bottom.

'Wullie!'

It was the kind of bellowed summons no barman worth the title ignores, for it signifies drinkers in dire need. Wullie Urquhart was worth the title and moved dutifully among the ranks of glasses, raised eyebrows dark and thick as forests. He murmured:

'Five pints, five nips?'

'Big yins.' Rab confirmed the order.

Their host nodded sagely. Dark, balding, bearded, hunched, massive…sageness didn't become him. He sighed, a theatrical gale of a sigh.

'Well, that's three tongues loose. It was too quiet to last, I suppose. Shame really.'

He poured. Pockets were raked loudly for money. Wullie silenced them again:

'I'll miss the old haverer too, him and his tall tales and bit poems. And the lassie. She was so cool, that one, like she was biding her time, waiting, always waiting. Waiting for him if ye ask me. Ken what I think?'

Sammy perked up, anxious to know if it was what *he* was thinking. It wasn't.

'I think,' said Wullie, 'it was someone like her that Burns had in mind for Annie Laurie…her hair was like the raven, her neck was like the swan…eh boys? Aye I see your smirks. You all think yur poets now, eh? And I just pour the pints and the nips, eh? Well let me tell you this – I ken

Burns. The thing about him wiz, he wiz just like the rest of us. He wouldnae be out of place if he walked in here now…and surely you'll be your pint stowp and surely I'll be mine, eh boys? Anyway, this yin's on the hoose.'

Wullie didn't put things 'on the hoose' ever. Nor did he make speeches like that. Then he poured himself a whisky, a dram that would half-fill a goldfish bowl. He never did that either, not in working hours, which was most of the hours God sent. He raised his glass at the fire, then at his friends and worthiest clientele:

'To him and Bella and their daft wanderings.'

'Good Wullie,' said Chas, the endorsement of all of them.

Another silence, as the enormity of the morning caught them up. Walter broke it in a small voice, a stage whisper to Rab:

'He doesnae ken that much Burns. It wiz Walter Scott wrote "Annie Laurie".'

Then he hastened down the drink in case Wullie took offence and withdrew the remarkable offer. But Wullie was retreating to the bar, either not hearing or affecting not to hear, for no-one would spoil the best speech of his life.

Robert said:

'Mind the first time?'

And suddenly they were all talking at once. They were all grins and guffaws again, shouting each other down, the brotherhood restored for how could they not mind the first time? A Friday, October time wasn't it, freezing snow on the skyline already? The door opens and instead of the Sally Army woman with a can and the *War Cry*, in he walks, gray robe, hair like snow, face like old stretched leather. When he asks for a drink in that deep ping-pong voice of his you could hear the jaws drop all round the room.

Chapter 2

'The Wellbeing of Mountain People is my Purpose'

෴

MANY MEN WERE restless in those difficult days between the wars. Many a tramp and wanderer forsook downcast town and city lives and took to the lonely roads of the Scottish Highlands. Nature's quietude among the mountains was the certainty they craved through that least certain of times.

It was a hospitable land then, unsuspicious of travellers and their motives, ignorant of tourism. Simple truths held sway. A solitary wanderer could travel, eat and sleep, albeit primitively, for next to nothing. Next to nothing was what most of them had, but they judged that richer than the nothing they had left behind. Such a wanderer might pay his dues with a story, a song, gossip gleaned on the road. These might buy him a bite, a bed, a pair of old boots with an untrodden mile or two left in them.

Often, that mysterious grapevine that whispers among Highland places would travel before him, announcing his arrival at the next village or township or farm. But there was one wanderer who captivated the grapevine as much as he taxed its powers.

He was tall and larch-straight. White hair fell to his broad shoulders or bannered out behind him when he faced the wind 'like a white wing', said an old one who nodded courteously to him on a north coast cliff path. His body was agile and lean, his length of stride as full as a stag's. But his face looked older than his body for it had weathered under the stings of many winds. His long sealskin coat was gray and looked like a robe. His speech bounced strangely on wide vowels and hard gutturals, a voice sculpted by far northern shores, a voice that sprang on the craning ear of the grapevine with the rhythms and music you might have heard in the Shetland of a century before, an antiquated lilt. A few coastal villagers, old hauled-out mariners who once went whaling in northern oceans, swore it was Iceland they heard in his voice, others said no, it was Faroe, or Norway, or Spitzbergen. They agreed at least about the hemisphere, and that his eyes were the eerie ice-green of glaciers.

Then there were his stories.

Such stories! And with these he would spellbind uneasy hosts wherever he paused. Stories of northern places imprisoned by mountains in a way no Highland places are. They told of poets in mountain places. Often, they told of swans (fearful glances among a few old Highlanders at that, for it is the troubled lot of the aged and wise to see through the swan stories), swans that wove their flights through the lives of mortals and interwove with their very existences, mortal becoming swan, swan becoming mortal.

In one village after another, people shook their heads at these stories, but the grapevine was enthralled despite itself, and the wanderer was asked for them again and again wherever he paused on his journey south, always south.

The swan stories troubled them for reasons they were slow to acknowledge. Indeed, they may not have been able to articulate them at all, for the reasons were rooted deep and distant, inherited from earlier eras than theirs, eras when a swan was held to be the guardian of a human's mortal soul, that when man, woman or child died, their souls flew on immortally, within swans.

It was also held that swan could become mortal, that changelings – poor enslaved creatures – walked the land between swan flightings. So you never turned away nor gave offence to the swan-folk. You could never be sure, and there was no way of knowing.

To add to the unease some felt, the Wanderer seemed to arrive in the landscape unpredictably, eluding the instincts of the grapevine, confounding its best guesses, troubling that fine line that skirts the frayed edge of folklore and unchancy eye-witness. So half-submerged instincts stirred strangely.

Sometimes the Wanderer would use the old ways through the hills that people had trod for as long as there had been people. But at other times he would pass through a landscape unseen and then some would say he had travelled by night and some say he flew, and both were the hallmarks of the swan-folk.

From Strathy Point on Scotland's northmost shore to Strathyre in Perthshire near the southmost beginning and end of the mountains, his travels held to their relentless southerly course. That too was curious, for it suggested he had the purpose of destination, whereas the wandering was destination enough for most of the Highlands' wayfarers.

They still say in Strathyre that it was an old hill shepherd, who had travelled the world's mountains himself and fetched up on that Highland Edge to while away his last years, who determined the ultimate course of events that befell the Wanderer. But all up and down the course of the Wanderer's travels through Scotland, the old ones who saw him said his destination was predetermined and beyond his control. That he was driven. And that too was the way things were for the swan-folk, or so the old handed-down stories told it.

Yet there is some persuasive evidence that the old shepherd passed the time of day with him on a hill shoulder west of the village a bit. The Wanderer, it seems, had taken to the high ground again, stag-striding out along that south-bound shoulder, shunning the easier going along Loch Lubnaig. If you had heard the story of that portentous meeting told by the Strathyre folk for a generation or two after the event, you would gather that the old shepherd had a good ear for the grapevine, and might have greeted the Wanderer thus:

'So, still south is it?'

'Still south,' the Wanderer smiled.

'Well, if you're holding south all day, and you're as thirled to the mountains as I think you are, there is only one left after this wee hill shoulder.'

He pointed to where a singular cone stood slightly aloof from all that landscape, the first and last mountain of the Highlands.

'What is its name, this signposting mountain?' the Wanderer asked.

'Ben Ledi.'

'Ledi? A strange name for a southern mountain. What does it mean?'

The shepherd shrugged.

'It's obscure now. Some swear it means the Mountain of God, others the Mountain of Light.'

'And what do you say? You must know it as well as anyone. God or Light?'

'I say it's much the same thing. All we can ask of our gods is that they shed a little light on the road ahead.'

The Wanderer smiled again, and added, 'Indeed. Or the road behind?'

'That can be useful too. Frankly a good light is more use to me than any god I ever heard of.'

The Wanderer, you may be sure, had a thoughtful ear for the conversation of the local people he met along the way, hearing them as eagerly as they heard his stories. He saw in them, it would seem, some kind of last hope for the mountain realm, a hope of guardianship. He had told the Strathyre folk (and doubtless many others on his way south):

'The wellbeing of mountain people is my purpose on the road. That and the wellbeing of the mountain.'

That afterthought had baffled as many as it intrigued. The shepherd, though, had heard it the night before in the village inn, heard the note of kinship it struck in him, and he saw now the quickening of this Wanderer's interest. He said:

'Mine is a seeing job. A good light breaks up the contours into watchable fragments. The hidden ledges are revealed where a beast might stand or fall, or an eagle nest or a fox lie up. Mostly there is good light in these mountains. A god, forever peering down through the clouds, is in no position to assist, for all that I ask one often enough.'

'And what do you do,' asked the Wanderer, 'if your seeing reveals a nesting eagle or a lying-up fox?'

'Do? I watch, of course. I watch how *they* see. They – the eagle and the fox in that order – are the best at the seeing job in the mountains. It may be, of course, that they do not see as far *back* as swans.'

'Shepherd,' said the Wanderer, smiling again, 'it has been good to talk to you. You are an extraordinary shepherd for such a land as this. What is your name?'

The shepherd nodded formally:

'John Muir, at your service.'

'I have heard of a John Muir who was a shepherd and poet of the mountains, although I hardly expected to meet him here.'

'As I hardly expected to find a swan-pilgrim. The swan things have been submerged longer than the wolf. People are unsure, now that you have let the light of swanflight into their eyes. The old ones know the stories. The young ones scoff. They will take some convincing. But I think I see what is at work within you. Wherever your journey leads, I hope there is a Light or a God – whatever pleases you – to illuminate the next good mile and the next. And a strong white wing when you need uplifting.'

The glacier-green eyes of the Wanderer turned on the one mountain shape which still lay to the south.

'The Mountain of Light. There can surely be no better place to let it end.'

The mountain commands all that land.

It stands at the throat of a pass, the first and last thoroughfare of the Highlands. It marks a watershed of landscapes. Near its summit lies a small watersheet, Lochan nan Corps, which is the Small Loch of the Corpse. A child's body was found in the lochan amid a great smothering of swan feathers. It was said in that land that he had been claimed by the swan folk, and that in many guises (but mostly as a single whooper swan – the Icelandic race that winters in Scotland) he still returned to the lochan during the quiet hours of dusk and dawn when he might linger secure from human gaze, mourning that which was lost.

The Wanderer came late in the afternoon to the lochan, a solitary figure on the back of the mountain landscape. For an hour, he stood there and only his coat and his hair moved in the wind. He looked as rooted as a tree or a heron. His silence matched his immobility. Then he climbed to the last mountain summit and there he thanked his own light-shedding God, for he believed at that moment he had been delivered from a great torment.

He had only ever known mountain lands, locked in places of the northlands of the earth where ice was still as much of an element as rock and wind and water and fire. Now he saw a broad river valley, its rich, harvested fields a chequer of gold in the lowering autumn sun. A long wall of low, flat-topped hills held the valley to the south, and where the valley opened to the east he saw where fields and river yielded to the supremacy of a single mighty rock. There the sun stoked pale fires in the surmounting walls of a great castle.

That rock drew him. His was an eye long accustomed to reading landscapes, so that it could penetrate the inscapes which are the unseen skeletal structures and foundations within and beneath all landscapes. Just as a good architect might gaze on a great building and marvel at the unseen genius of its construction, as well as the beauty of its façade, so he could comprehend the hand of nature as architect in the midst of its great works.

So he appraised the far-off rock and its flat-bottomed river valley thus:

'First the volcano spat and roared and cloaked itself in heaps of its own spoil, then cooled. Then it shed its useless, loosening, outer layers and reinvented itself, cold and alone, the naked rock.

'Next the ice, the great ice that carved the valley but baulked at the cold rock, gripped it but could not overwhelm it.

'Next the sea. These two, ice and sea, nature's foremost designers, shaped the waist of this land. The ice melted, the sea flowed and flowed until it acknowledged an unyielding mountain chain, these mountains where I stand, a protecting arm about the waist.

'The sea relented. As it withdrew eastwards, it also deferred to the one cold rock in all the valley. That rock remains, the volcano's souvenir, hewn and coughed up out of the valley's oldest darkness. The ice was too new, and no match for it. But neither was the sea, and that is more remarkable, for it is rare in an island landscape for a rock to wear down the sea.

'So the sea parted, swam round the rock, fell back and back. Now, instead of the ice, instead of the sea, a water snake swims, a great river, deep and dark and coiled. Its strength is fed by the benevolence of these mountains, its kin, for they too were once the ice's tortured prisoners, worn and wearied down to the nub.

'Men came.

'Where the sea had fallen back they found the valley, fertile and sheltered by mountainside and hillside. They would marvel at the one cold rock, at its command of the country in all directions, at its prospects to the mountains, at the great river below it (their safe passage to and from the sea whence they had come). Was there a sounder place in all the land to fortify and settle? There was none. So they claimed the rock for their own, built a wooden fortress there, then a succession of bigger and better wooden fortresses, then that great stone castle that still stands, then a walled town that spilled downhill from the plinth to a bridge over the river, a causeway beyond the bridge across the sodden valley to the foothills, to the mountains beyond.'

So that was the rock the Wanderer set eyes on from the summit of the Mountain of Light, twenty miles distant. The rock had long since been named according to its own story – Stirling. But once it was called Strivelin, which is the Place of Strifes, after all the warrings of nature the rock had endured. It would prove a prophetic name as well as a historic one, for in the agonising birth throes, life throes and death throes of Scotland, the independent nation, the rock watched a parade-ground of battlefields assemble and wither away in its shadow, licking its myriad wounds.

If you held the rock and its castle, you held the key to the kingdom, or so men thought once, but the key to their Scotland was never so simple as that, and it has long since rusted in the unfathomable lock of the Union, all but immovable and more elusive than ever.

In the river valley and its one cold rock, the Wanderer saw and sensed a change in the land. It was as the shepherd Muir had told him. There was no mountain beyond, and he sensed that the values and priorities that are common to all mountain lands would also be absent. In their place, what...? Perhaps it was then he saw a white ripple go through the gold swathe of fields and knew it for a skein of whooper swans, for the Icelandic whoopers fall from the wide fire of the valley's autumn skies and linger winter-long. The birds' presence might have reassured him, so that when he went down at last he would go eagerly, down to the valley that its people called the Carse.

From the Carse the rock, the Place of Strifes, beckoned peacefully enough. There, he reasoned, the Highland grapevine would have lost its thread, for the place stood alone in its own realm, neither Highland nor Lowland, and walled in only by the distant flanks of the Carse, the low hills to the south, the mountains to the north. Whatever else, it would be a place with its own story, its own strifes.

An Old Crone's words were in his ears as he climbed down and felt the floor of the Carse flatten under his feet, words from a distant time, a distant mountain land:

'Absorb all that the mountains can give you, but then stand for a winter beyond the furthest edge of the mountains. Cross that bridge of landscapes. See the mountains with the eyes of those who live beyond.'

Chapter 3

'A Man with a Thirst and No Money Cannot Afford to Take Offence Either'

⬦⬦⬦

SO I LOOKED long and quiet at Rab and Bella and the others, saw their firelight faces and remembered. Remembered the sky-fire mountains over my shoulder that first night I climbed the paths and streets of the rock, weary and wondering. Wondering at the old castle and its coat-tails town, at the dark, cold rock itself, its impenetrable bulk, wondering at my own presence here, my own uncertainty in the face of that great rock-certainty.

It was a gray place after all nature's autumn brightness among the woody fields of the Carse and the relaxed pace of the river. But snow clouds had settled on the suddenly distant mountains, covering my tracks as I saw it, shutting me out from my own domain, pushing me down into the shadow of the rock. Climbing up through the town, it had felt as if the rock had once inhaled a great breath centuries ago and incarcerated it, a cold lung. Poised and pent-up, it held its breath still, and the effort of that great containment spread through the gray streets, the gray houses, to the gray folk themselves. It must be said, it was a town smothered in rags and hard times.

I climbed steep, narrow streets until I found the inn that stood above the town on a projecting shelf of the rock, and hard under the castle like an oblivious rabbit beneath a spreadeagle of dark wings. The windows of two walls squinted at the mountains. A wind-creaking, rust-and-iron sign proclaimed "The Castle Inn". It looked ancient and forlorn, but in reality it was only ancient. I took a deep breath, pushed at a heavy oak door, walked into a room thronged with drinkers, asked the innkeeper for a drink and said I would pay for it with a story.

The innkeeper threw back a black acre of beard so that it almost pointed at the ceiling and he roared. It was a gesture calculated to attract the attention of every drinker in the room and of course it worked at once. His mockery found a chorus in almost every throat in the room. He'd heard some outrageous ways of trying to evade his "nae credit" rule, he said, ingenious some of them, and he thought he'd heard them all. But a story for a pint – no, that was new. He turned on me then with black, unsmiling eyes and said:

'And what kind of story did ye have in mind? A ghost story, I dare say, for yur the nearest thing to a ghost that's darkened this place for a wheen o centuries.'

To be fair, I must have cut a bizarre figure in my trail-weariness, for this was a room unaccustomed to passing travellers. The black eyes handed me an empty glass.

'Tell you what. Gie wiz yur ghost story and ye can have this. It's the ghost o a pint.'

I held still while the laughter flowed, then ebbed. A man with a thirst and no money cannot afford to take offence either. I looked round at so so many strange and smirking faces, then found my eye held by one more smile, this one in a small, aloof group who sat in a rough circle at the fire. I repeated my request, told the room that my stories had been my currency all through Scotland from the northmost shore to here, but maybe there was no appetite for stories and hospitality beyond the mountains? The smiling face rose from its fireside cameraderie and crossed the room. Then that same Rab, who in a single winter has become my dearest friend, put a shilling on the bar, and when his grin had subsided enough to get the words out, he said:

'If you're as drouthy as that, Neebor, it's on me, and bring yur story to the fire away from this illiterate bear of an innkeeper. He'd throw out Robert Burns if he walked in here without the price of a pint on him.'

'Aye,' countered the bear, 'and if word got oo' that Wullie Urquhart was sellin pints for the price o a poem, every other buggar in the Tap o the Toon'd be cryin himself Rabbie an slaverin aboo' mooses.'

The banter crossed the bar with the coin and the beer and the laughter. I thanked my benefactor, drank his health with a traveller's relish, considered him over the rim of the glass. He was younger, square, dark, confident, at ease, at home, but behind the eyes I sensed the stillness of a man weary with conflict, another striver in the Place of Strifes. Does that sound fanciful? Such a snap judgment at first glance? A first glance, at that, among such a throng of unfamiliar faces?

It is only the judgment of an eye that has had to learn to be quick, the eye of a beggar-who-would-be-chooser. But I sat by that fire all winter, and the more I returned Rab's rock-still gaze, the more that judgment rang true.

He led me back to the hearth that first night and introduced Chas, Robert, Walter, Sammy, Bella, the four men hewn from the same dark rock as himself, the woman different, somehow displaced, a swan among geese. They shifted their chairs to accommodate me in their circle. I thought of the grazing geese out on the afternoon Carse. As each new incoming skein spilled the air from its wings and skidded down to the field, the grazing pack shuffled and made way for the incomers. Now these six accommodated my arrival down from the mountain air. I was an incoming skein. They shuffled their small pack and made way.

I remember it all.

I remember all that they have done for me, these people and their rock-clinging town, and I will not forget. I will remember forever, which in my many lives means exactly what it says. One day, somehow, I will find a way to repay it all. Keep my chair warm, Neebors.

But now I find, scanning this recollection, that I have not told the very first story of all, the one which paid for my first drink in the back bar of the Castle Inn.

Chapter 4

The Wanderer's First Story – The Grace
of the Mountain

ৎৡৱ৩

I AM TIED umbilically to the mountains, spilled among them from the womb, child of their parentage.

It was in the mountains I rooted, it was on the mountains' milk that I was weaned. We belong mutually, the mountains and I. We are fragments of the same landscape. I may not be hewn by glaciers, or coughed up by volcanoes, and they are granite-and-saxifrage, not blood-and-bone. But there is mountain-ness in my veins and my heart, and the rhythm of the mountain heart is a pulse that matches my own.

I see your scepticism. You think, perhaps, that the mountain has no heart? I think it has. But then I was taught to believe that all nature has. And not just one heart but two. Here is a poem to the two hearts of nature. (At this point you could have seen an uneasy ripple cross the firelight faces – a poem! – as though a fox had stepped softly into the edge of the goose field.)

Nature beats out time
with two interlocking hearts.
One's only for the ears of gods
– and glaciers in their day –
resounding in mighty silence
of stone and ice, mountain
and ancient pine,
the clan of stoics.

The other's the lesser heart
nature wears on the sleeves
of all her gowns,
audible to all heart-seekers
attuned to any alpine lady's mantle.

A pause. An intense silence, not comfortable. Perhaps it was too soon for poems? But a poem had been spoken, in the back bar of the Castle Inn, a poem not Burns. It had not even rhymed. I looked at the faces. Rab frowned. Walter scratched his head, vaguely embarrassed. Robert and Chas swallowed it whole, indistinguishable from a mouthful of beer. Sammy nodded. Bella smiled and seemed to like it. Chas belched, said "I don't get it but we'll let it pass," a gentle admonition for the committed sin of poetry on his territory, then swallowed more beer.

Sammy said:

'Alpine lady's mantle's a flower. You get it on the Ben, lots of wee leaves, silver underneath…they shine when the wind blows.'

Robert said:

'A flower. That's clever.'

But his face was a blank page.

Rab was feeling short-changed and urged on the story, determined to protect his investment.

For forty years, I said, the mountains and I grew older in each other's company, the shadow of the one falling across the substance of the other. On the winter mountain I am as the white hare, the ptarmigan, the arctic fox, thirled to snows, still as the white rock. Autumns and springs I migrate down and up the mountain, old gold and new green as the birches. Summers I linger high and pant away the heat.

These are chameleon ways with the mountain landscape. But the chameleon is limited. It does not, for example, try to match the *mood* of the mountain. That is something perhaps only a poet would dare.

Poets are a powerful and revered force in my land, even the living ones. They are listened to eagerly. Bardic traditions run deep within the mountain villagers, where wildest nature has a godly presence. But poets are also subjected to the burdens of the tradition. It is a rigid framework within which they must strive, reworking ancient themes. A wise old woman of my land once wrote:

'A poet's work is to lower a spider-thread into the black void between rocks whence comes sea-music, and record vibrations reaching his fingertips, to lift hairs on the neck, songs in the heart's ear.'

But there is one yet more onerous burden to the tradition, unique to the poets of my land. It is this: if the poet is ever found lacking, if his work is so seriously questioned that his adherence to the tradition is in doubt (it is his decision alone – self-scrutiny is the only law that regulates the lives of poets), he must make an arduous pilgrimage into the furthest mountain wilderness where few human feet ever tread. The purpose is to pare away the layers of useless status that might have accumulated over the years, so that they dull or even blind the poet's perception; to seek the simplest and deepest truths that only wilderness solitude can teach and that perhaps only the poet can hear; to learn to think as the mountain thinks; to return at last and pass on the new knowledge to his people.

I feel these things keenly. I am such a poet, on just such a pilgrimage.

There came a day when a stranger walked into our crowded village inn, much as I have just walked into yours. That inn was my stage, and the villagers would gather there often to hear poems and stories. That evening, I was giving new poems and threading them together with ideas and stories, strands of the same ancient web in which we are all held, we northland poets...of nature, of mountains, of swans, of voyages, of great bards. My people love the endless exploration of these themes, for we are taught that there are no new themes, only new ways of considering old themes, new ways to navigate among ancient rocks. But the stranger heard these things with disapproval as blatant as a bruise on a fair face.

It is good to have strangers in our midst from time to time. Mountain villages are such locked-in places. The presence of strangers can often stimulate, challenge and confirm our values. They remind us, too, of our obligations of hospitality, and accordingly I invited him into the discussion of old truths. But instead, he branded me loudly as a liar and an arrogant one at that. Those were his very first words in our company. But then he yelled:

'I will tell you what I do not hear. I do not hear your humility. I find no hint of it. There is no greater virtue in the mountains than humility. You seem to me to lack it utterly. You bring shame on your place and your people and your traditions. Your clever words disguise nothing, because compared to the great poets you have just named, you *are* nothing.'

A voice from the throng of my compatriots said:

'Friend, you have the air of a Lowlander. What do you really know of the mountains?'

It was a calm question, doubtless intended to calm the man so that he might reconsider his outburst, but he purpled and raged back:

'And what do you really know of Lowlanders? You do not need to be born among mountains to know their worth. You are not the only ones who feel for the mountains. They are not *your* mountains.'

A second, angrier villager voice:

'I think you are a townsman who comes to the mountains to be briefly a fish out of water.'

And a third:

'Yes, and a fish out of water has need of humility.'

The laughter inflamed him.

'What do you know of the world beyond your safe and shut-off havens? What other poets do you hear? What other music but your own dreary dirges? None! You close yourselves in and make a virtue out of it, but the truth is it shrivels the scope of your minds. Look out there! Look beyond your mountain noses.

'The rest of the world – yes, the Lowland world…the world of forest and foothill and plain and marsh and moorland and desert, the world of the sea – does not see the mountains as you do, as enclosing, defining things, but rather as liberating things, the wildest imaginable, the greatest liberation of all save perhaps the sea.

'Did any of you ever shut yourself in the sea like an islander? Have you ever even seen the sea? You think your mountains are the beginning and the end of the world, and you praise a mountain poet like, like…*this!*

'I think you have grown deaf with too many mountain winds!'

The mood in the room darkened. We are a hospitable tribe, but we are fierce in defence of our own kind and our own world. We have known too many intrusions from beyond the mountains through too many eras, when the motives of the intruders have threatened our ways. Yet I felt partly responsible for the situation that had arisen. I made another attempt to reason with the stranger, to show him our perspective of the mountain world from within. I told him:

'The difference is that being born among mountains we can be easy in their company. That is rarely given to those who first see the mountains from afar. We look at the mountains and we see ourselves. We are the blood. The mountains are the bone. We learn by the growth of instinct as well as by the example of our elders, to match the mountain challenges as they match ours. So it does not do to be small in their company. Not insignificant. No, not *humble*. It is no humble thing to be born here, to live a life here, to die here, then go on among mountains, in eternal renewal.

'There is no humility in the ptarmigan or the saxifrage. They know techniques of survival here only because they have evolved to match challenge after challenge with eggs and buds, broods and blooms. In that respect, we are no different. Each greets the mountain every day according to its mood and the mountain's mood, and thrives on the common ground between its mood and the mountain's mood. So it is with us.

'If the Tall Ones are buoyed and brightened by sunny winds, spring your step with them. If the mountain fire is smoored by mists, dribbling rains, clenched clouds, go deep and dark and cool yourself. You cannot fool the mountain by whistling when it asks for silence, but can you out-silence the mountain?

'It is no shame to go downcast among mountains, no defeat. No insult to them if you happen to be ungrateful for the climbing. What matters is to be of the landscape as you find it.

'Humility? No. It has no part in it.'

Smiles and raised glasses at that from my friends! Their mood eased, but the stranger's did not. He was unmoved and unrepentant and he seized on my use of the words, "Tall Ones".

'That very phrase is an admission of your inferiority. It is a concession to the mountain! The tradition that confers such a title on the mountains implies humility at the very least, even if you as an individual place yourself above it.'

So I explained that in the language of our mountain tribe, the single word that best translates – however inadequately – as "Tall Ones" has many inferences. The adults of the tribe are Tall Ones and the elders among the adults are distinguished in the same way. Its specific meaning is always clear from its context. The stallions of our wild horses, the dog fox, the female eagle (being larger than her spouse) – they are all Tall Ones. Once I heard an old man call the arcs of a double rainbow Tall One and Taller One, but he was an exceptional linguist.

So the mountain village has its Tall Ones in the surrounding peaks. Distant mountains may be higher, but they are diminished by their distance and exert a lesser influence. Once the theme of the conversation is established, the Tall Ones are the dominant influences within the theme at that moment.

It was then that a voice in the throng cried:

'Well spoken, Tall One!'

The bridge I had been trying so carefully to build towards the Lowlander collapsed at that moment. The words galvanised him. He rounded on me furiously.

'Ah, so you too are proclaimed "Tall One"! Is that because of your status as a poet or your supreme swagger? What are you? Mountain god? Moses back from Sinai brandishing immortal words? No – these are not tablets of stone you brandish, Tall One.'

He made a sneer of the words.

'They are worthless rubble, less worth than the ash spewn from the volcano.'

There was an ominous ugliness in the man now. He had grown volcanic himself. There was fire in his belly and he had begun to erupt. I would have been wiser to let his storm of rage blow itself out. But my people had thrown a gladiatorial arena around us. They expected me to confront his ugliness with fine words, with the traditions of our language, to counter him not just with eloquence but with barbs here and there so that occasionally the words startle and sting. They were angry at the Lowlander, and they wanted a showdown.

I told him:

'There was a great poet before me. But he judged himself wanting and made a great pilgrimage from which he did not return, so we could not learn from the new knowledge he might have gleaned from his pilgrimage. After twenty-one years, the stipulated time according to our tradition, I inherited his mantle. I try to be the best poet I can, as true to our landscape traditions as I can. I wear the burdens of the tradition as lightly as I can.

'I am, I concede, one of the fortunate ones, being a mountain poet. So many who are born to the mountains find no work, take to the Lowland towns and sever the umbilical ties, and so begin to die a little each day. They breathe only the sour Lowland air to which they were not born, to which neither their lungs nor their heart are fitted. They grow deaf to the step of the doe on the moss, blind to the fall of an eagle shadow across a high crag. I grieve for them, the lost ones, and write often of their sufferings, for they all suffer. I count the blessings that attend my pen and let me stay.

'My work flows out of the mountains and through my people and there it begins and there it ends, a glacier of words. It is for them that I write. I do not write for Lowland ears. I cannot. Some say that limits the work. I say: who commands a bigger stage than this? And throw a gesture of my arms at the scope of the mountains.

'From time to time, an academic from some distant university crosses the mountain pass in search of our primitive literacy to try and give it wider meaning – its themes are universal enough. But however diligent and gifted he may be, there is much he will not understand for all his learning, because there is much the mountains will not give him to understand.'

The Lowlander stirred himself again from his brandy gloom.

'How do you measure yourself now, *Tall One*, now that there are no contemporaries or critics to judge your work?' he asked.

The question startled me, for although it was more taunt than question in his mouth, I have asked myself the same question many times. It had been too long since the last gathering of poets from all that mountain country's valleys. In too many valleys, the bloom of the people has withered. These valleys have wildered as the hearthstones have grown cold. As valley after valley has grown still, the hearths smokeless, the homes childless (it is always the absence of children you notice first, for the child-bearing age is always the first to leave the valley, always the first...) so the distance between bards has grown.

The valleys are like links in an ancient chain, the chain of the tradition. The chain is incomplete. There are many breaks. There is nothing more useless than a fragmented chain. It will be my business from now to forge new links, reunite fragments, so that the chain of the tradition can be secure again, in time, in time.

So, it does not do for a poet to be too long outwith the company of others who comprehend that most tensile of trades, for in permanent isolation the thing grows more and more taut until it gives. And nor does it do to have your work fall only on the ears of your champions. Criticism by your peers – those who stand at the heart of your tradition – whether pointed or pointless, trivial or enlightened, or (the rarest of all) an unqualified hosanna, is a crucial component of self-judgment. It had been too long. I had listened too long to the adulation of my own people.

All this I considered silently, and in much less time than it takes to tell, as the Lowlander's question sank in. I was about to defend myself, urged on by my people's confident expectation, when I realised that he knew I would have a prepared response. Even as I began to speak, I wondered how long I had been protecting myself from this moment. I recognised the Lowlander's trap, even as I stepped into it. I began:

'I measure myself most clearly against the starry saxifrage, and for this reason. The first of these I ever saw (as a child of four – see how a single mountain flower shines through a life!) was deep in a natural tomb high on a mountainside where I walked with my father. It was a cool, dark chamber in which the saxifrage was a glow worm. It struck me then to be a huge dwelling place for such a tiny flowers. There was room – I hazard now a frantic guess – for a million such flowers in that chamber, but there was only one flower there because there were only enough natural resources there to sustain one. I say: can I amount to a saxifrage in my airy mountain chamber; can I draw on the wilderness enough to provide sustenance for one pure flowering?'

More smiles in that room! More raised glasses from my friends, a new tumbler of rum at my elbow! But the Lowlander turned into the lamplight with his eye afire. The long table trembled under such a tumult of fists that every glass either spilled or fell over, yet neither the spilled drink nor the new and vivid ire of the drinkers seemed to register with the man in his fury. And to the punctuation of his fists on that flooded, wooden plain, his words hit home:

'To measure yourself by a saxifrage is to blaspheme before the mountain gods! To deny humility in your mountain life is to belittle the power that created the saxifrage and commanded it to shine! Your wit and your words are nothing without the humility to defer to the company of mountains, deer, ptarmigan, titmouse, even a saxifrage, even a pinewood ant! The mountain pulls down clouds and fashions snows and storms from them. Where are your snows and storms, Tall One? Write me a snowdrift! The deer seek out the shelter of the forest in the storm while you flee *from* the forest to your four walls and your fire! The ptarmigan hatches out on the very summits so that the young are the true heirs of the mountain! How far *down* the mountain were you born, Tall One?'

The villagers were growing angrier, shifting their feet, putting down glasses heavily, freeing hands for trouble, but still the Lowlander's assaults poured out, an unstoppable flow, the eruption at its climactic height:

'Saxifrage and ant toil night and day through every living moment the mountain permits by its grace. How well and wisely do you toil, Tall One? Do you call this posturing in front of your kinsmen *toil?* These games with words...*toil?*

'Or are you killing time? As if you could kill time without injuring eternity! Do you know that sentiment? Thoreau. Do you know Thoreau? No, of course not. He only lived with a pond, not an encirclement of mountains! What could a low-life pond-dweller have to say to a mountain man? Why would you want the wisdom of sunlight to permeate your mountain darkness?

'That is the limitation of life lived forever among mountains. You spend too much time among shadows! How well do you think you sit in the eye of the mountain's grace, Tall One?'

His words hit me like bullets. My friends saw me in invincible armour when it came to skirmishes of language. He saw clear through to the unprotected heart. He aimed a last wound:

'The mountain can avalanche away your whole village, your whole valley. Can you avalanche away the mountain with your absence of humility and your stockpile of words? Go on, Tall One, write me an avalanche, write me the faith that moves mountains. Tall One – ha! I believe I just saw you shrink!'

A hand smothered the stranger's mouth from behind. More hands seized his arms and held them behind his back. My people had had enough. He was howled down and silenced and ushered none too gently out into the night. The villagers' tolerances had been worn through. How well they all rallied to me that night, filled glass after glass for me. But an ocean of rum could not have drowned the man's words or dulled their pain.

I spent a fearful night. Sleep was fitful and fouled by dark dream.

Dream planted a name in the front of my mind, a name I knew as well as my own, the haunting, dark monsyllable of my great predecessor, the bardic hero of three generations before my own. Rolf. It was said of me that I had his glacier-green eyes. Dream showed me those eyes, but placed them in the face of the Lowlander. The sight appalled me. The eyes of Rolf were my inheritance; I had heard that said again and again by the elders in the village, those who knew Rolf well. But if Rolf was abroad in the hereafter without his eyes, where would be his visions? Without his visions, my own wellspring would be dry, bereft of the pure waters of continuity.

My duty, as dream saw it, was clear. I must retrieve Rolf's eyes so that we both might see again. I clawed at the Lowlander's face, but it simply came closer to me so that my hands reached too far beyond him, and I could only meet the advance of the eyes with my own gaze from inches away. I saw then the reflection of the inn fire in the eyes, the red dance of the flame at the very heart of the glacier green, fire and ice, the shapers of the land. Occasionally, the flame's dance would slow and whiten as though a third force was struggling to emerge from within that collaboration of fire and ice. Finally the flame stilled and the white force emerged in the shape of a swan's wing. I struck again at that stranger-face, and prised the eyes free. At once my own eyes were in my own hands and through them I could look back from my hands at my own sightless face. I restored my eyes and the face before me became woman, a woman with long dark hair to her waist.

The last thing I remember before I awoke was the song she sang. When I did awake I wrote it down at once. If I were to translate it out of the ancient northern tongue that sang it, it would say:

In the filmy cloud-white morning
Three swans flew eastward, an arrow
Fired at the sun. One
The swan of time past. Two
The swan of the present. Three
The swan of the unknowing
Hereafter.

Three swans! In the Northlands the Three Nornes – the Fates representing past, present and future – appear to mortal eyes as three swans.

In the morning, I went to the house of the Crone. She is a kind of tribal elder, a matriarch, of great age and as wise as she is old. She had chosen to live a little apart from the village by then, a little higher up the mountain, so that to visit her was to be aware of ascending towards a more rarified place, a more isolated presence. Her house was simple and single-roomed and quite devoid of ornament. There was a single shelf of old books, no more than twenty of them, but all of them much thumbed, much patched-up and repaired. They were the works of mountain poets all across the Northlands. She once told me:

'I have no use for new ideas now. I deal only with those masters who set down great and simple truths. There *are* no new ideas, only the old ideas of the masters dressed in new clothes.'

So she read and reread her few books and travelled in her mind, along paths of eloquence, leaving me to wonder if it could ever be enough for a writer like myself to aspire to anything more than a set of new clothes. I was much younger then and quite hurt by the idea, although I knew better than to disagree with her. I see now that she was urging me to accept no limitations, to listen to no-one's opinion about what I was capable of other than my own. Having learned that, the quest for a new idea, a new truth, is the great elusive, the unattainable, and therefore the impetus for a life's work. To be told by one so wise as the Old Crone that it does not exist is to be told that nothing matters other than the search to find it, for the searching will draw forth all that there is in you to draw. Or at least that is how I chose to interpret her.

That morning after my troubling dream, she was expecting me, though God knows how. She had not been at the inn and could have had no other visitor between the events of the night before and my arrival. Yet she seemed to know the detail of what had taken place, to understand with a certainty that was far beyond anything she could have gleaned from casual gossip. She was a hub of many insights that travelled to her through the mountain valleys, fleet as winds.

'There was an unnerving man at the inn,' I told her. 'His words were wounds. He had come sufficiently armed to wound.'

She nodded and asked how she could help me, 'Tall One', she added and at once restored to the words the reassurance of dignity, healing at last that which they had suffered from the Lowlander's taunts.

'Tell me about Rolf,' I said.

Her face arched in surprise.

'Rolf! But surely you have studied him all your life since the first poet-inklings were discerned in you?'

'Studied his work, yes, always his work…but the man…I know almost nothing of the man.'

She tutted, and muttered an oath against teachers today.

'As if you could understand the words without knowing of the man…And something in the stranger has put Rolf in your mind?'

I told her the dream. I have never been one to place much faith in dreams. Dreams have always seemed to me to be nothing more than a convenient means of emptying the mind of the day's accumulated rubbish. But this one had been such a dark and forceful thing. I feared it.

She was quiet for a long time, so long that I began to wonder if she had heard me properly, but then I saw in her eyes that in considering her answer she had to travel a very great distance, though whether in time or miles I could not say. So I waited while her mind travelled. At last she said:

'Rolf…knew his limitations.'

It was hardly the revelation I was hoping for. After a pause, she added:

'Or perhaps he feared them. But he worked exceptionally well within them. He worked the same few themes again and again, as you will know, always mining the same old seams, always finding new riches there.'

She smiled suddenly, remembering, a smile that wiped fifty years from her face.

'Once he talked to me for half a day about "the Grace of the Mountain" – that was one of his themes. It was the most beautiful thing I ever heard from a human mouth. You may win such grace when you have lived through enough, if you are willing to suffer enough, for it is not lightly won. Anyway, such understanding is, perversely enough, not unknown among Lowlanders.'

'Rolf was a Lowlander?!'

She seemed surprised that I did not know. Surely…from my studies…?

'Only his words were ever made available to me, so that I should recognise only their worth, not his flaws. My tutors…'

'*Flaws!* Is that what your tutors told you? Tutors! Pah! Experts on great writers who have never written a line that amounts to so much as sparrow droppings. Flaws! Ach…'

She silenced herself, editing her own outrage. She calmed herself and continued:

'It is no "flaw" to be a Lowlander, although I think perhaps he thought that it was too. Or perhaps he was told it was a flaw. Maybe by a tutor.

'Perhaps you would know – surely his words would give this away – that he worshipped our wild swans?'

'Worshipped?'

'Yes, it is the right word.'

She shook her head sadly

'Swans! As if we did not have gods enough. He used to get so depressed because he did not share their birthright. At times you could see behind his beautiful eyes that monumental stillness that marks a man weary with conflict.

'He had come to the mountains as a very young child, but always, for all his gifts and all his industry, the fact of his distant birthplace – in Scotland – unbalanced him. The older he grew, the more it troubled him. At last his work grew poor, and when he left to make the pilgrimage, he was already a broken man. It is not a thing for a broken man to undertake. I knew he would never return.'

'Never?'

She shook her head. Her lips were thin as the hardest mountain skyline edge. They say he died two years later, she said, some glacier or other up north tipped him into a crevasse. Then she brightened:

'He had a power! He could penetrate an argument, unnerve the most confident of opponents, although his technique would not always win admirers. But the power of it always thrilled me! He was severe with anyone he considered to be failing themselves, not fulfilling their potential. He worked his limits to the utmost, you see, he over-reached and outstripped his own potential. He insisted on living for...what was his phrase?...oh, I heard it so often...you must forgive an old, done woman...ah! I remember! *every living moment the mountain permits by its grace!*'...that was it!'

I asked her:

'You say he died. Are you sure of that?'

She shrugged. 'With great poets,' she said, 'what does a death matter?'

A dam burst in my head. Reason drowned. She saw the one certainty that was left for me, the one my tradition demanded.

'If you make the pilgrimage,' she said, 'absorb all that the mountains can give you, then stand for a winter beyond the furthest edge of the mountains. Cross that bridge of landscapes. See them with the eyes of those who live beyond. Write that viewpoint too.'

She stood then, tall and slim and lithe for all her great age, and offered a kind of benediction:

'The Grace of the Mountain go with you, Tall One.'

Those were her last words to me.

So that was how I became a Wanderer. And that was twenty years ago, twenty years of living on my words and my wits. Twenty years among the mountains of the Northlands, travelling just below the ice where the Grace of the Mountain is at its purest. When the ice crept south in the winter, I would creep south before it. When it relented in summer, I tracked it north. But what began as a pilgrimage in search of a shed light became instead an obsession. For every mountain reveals the next mountain and the next mountain range. Perhaps it will be that next one that conceals the enlightenment…so you go on and on. The travelling becomes the day's work, arduous and addictive. Nights become an impatient lull before the next dawn, the next day's journey. The journey finally became its own purpose.

'Then I remembered the Old One's advice, to stand for a winter beyond the mountains, so I turned south, crossed the northern seas, and here I am.'

That was my first story before this fire, the one that bought me my first drink and won me the hearing of new friends, the one that ensured I could spend a winter here, in an attic room of the Castle Inn, facing north towards the distant mountains.

At the end of my story, when I sat back and spread my palms wide, no-one seemed to know how to react. Rab stared at me, wordless. Bella's eyes were on the fire. Chas drank, studying his glass. Walter's face was meaningless. Sammy was thinking, framing a question, and while he thought and framed, Robert spoke.

'Haye…' he said, labouring the start of the word with an intake of breath, the sound of it as meaningless as Walter's face. So Walter said:

'Aye what?'

'Aye, it was a good story. No true of course, but good. Ken this, Ah cannae mind the last time Ah sat doon and had someone tell iz a story. 'S good, eh?'

Sammy was still thinking, still working up to his question. They called him Futret – weasel – for his thin, pointed face and his thinning red hair and his dark eyes. And it seems to me, now that I know him better, that curiosity is a hunger in him, as it is in all weasels. At last…

'This Grace of the Mountain thing…what is it exactly? I mean, how do you recognise it? Just breathe it in? Or what? Or maybe you haven't found it? Maybe you don't know and you're still looking?'

And Chas added:

'And maybe it just breaks out all over your face like mumps, and that's how you know you've got it.'

Chas could put smirks back on all their faces. But I had that little posse of questions to answer, and they were looking at me again, wondering what I would make of them.

So I grinned back at Chas, noted that Rab's hard stare had eased off, then turned to Sammy:

'I would say, Sammy, that the thing I have learned is how to part the ways of other men, to step aside and go my own way, deeper into the landscape than just travelling through it. I…'

'Balls,' said Chas softly.

Rab glared at him. Bella put a finger to her lips. Neither gesture had any effect at all.

'It's balls,' he said again. 'Not a word of it makes sense. Part the ways of other men? Deeper into the landscape than jist traivellin through…whu' the…whu's that about?

'Come on Neebor…'

Then I heard in my head again the Crone say 'Flaws!', and Chas's 'Balls!' was the same exasperated rebuke. So I tried again.

'I would set myself challenges. Could I see the landscape, could I work with nature, the way a wild swan does? Could I use the senses – the eyes, say – of other creatures, like a deer, or an eagle, and so come closer to nature, and that way see more, and learn more, more about why nature is the way that it is? You learn the trick of it when you are a wanderer for a living.

'There are places…perhaps you part a screen of birches, or step aside into the shadow of an ancient pine that has stood where it still stands for 400 years, and you try and borrow from that rootedness. There are moments that turn your head in raw admiration – the flight of a skein of swans across the face of a mountain, or the downcurve of an eagle wingtip, or the way an otter flows without pause between rock and water. These things are keys to be turned. They let you deeper in. There *are* lands within lands. Unseen by most people, but sparsely populated by the tribe of wanderers, creatures whether man or swan or deer or eagle or otter, who leave no trace of passage, because they have begun to think like the mountain. Like wolves, they move at the edge of things.

'The Grace of the Mountain…think of a cloak you can never put off, an inner garment rather than an outer one, so that you wear it as you wear your skin, and you would no more walk in the mountains without the one than you would without the other.

'The more you walk among the mountains, looking, seeking, asking, the more the mountains give of themselves. Oh but they are such misers! They ask not only that you give everything, but also that you prise your reward (the reward? – the mountain's secrets!) from their strongest clasp. So you win, say, a sliver of rock's worth of insight for a traverse of a hundred miles. But you must make what you can of the slivers. Don't undervalue them, for what is an entire mountain range other than an amalgamation of rock slivers?

'And have I found the Grace of the Mountain? I think that there have been moments when I have felt as if I walked hand-in-glove with what I've been looking for.

'Am I still looking for it? Oh yes. And I always will be, for it is the code that runs my life.'

'Well you won't find it here,' Chas muttered. 'Ah think yur nuts, but you've got guts and you tell a good story. Beer?'

Chapter 5

The Dark Crouching Angel on the Shoulder of All of Us

⸙

IT WAS NEVER the tradition here, unlike my mountain valley, to pass the stories round the table with the rum bottle (the bottle pausing agreeably with each story-teller to loosen and lubricate his voice and vigour), but I have rarely met a warmer welcome than I was accorded that October night. I was a curio, of course, a wild man, something the mountain wind had blown in. But if you ever find a more hospitable folk than the natives of that rock-rooted town, you will have unearthed a tribe of saints. Not that they were all saints there! Every street had its drunks and wasters and thieves, but there was a proud core and a rough kindness within every man and woman I met, once we had peeled away the layers of armour they wear to fend off or kick back at life. A legacy of the strifes, no doubt.

What was strange was the way the story-telling caught on. Once it became no longer awkward to sit in a circle and listen to my haverings (ah, but there is art to the havering!) one of the six might put down a new tray of drinks and say:

'That reminds me a bit of the time when...' and something would emerge out of the recollection. Or one would goad another with 'Robert, you were there, mind the time we met the ghost of Sheriffmuir?' and Robert, if the mood was in him and the whisky fires well enough stoked, would mind fine. Minding fine was what the Rock folk did best: considering the stories incarcerated in the Rock's long story, there was much to mind. Slowly, over the weeks, recollection would become suffused with invention and ornament, and they would begin to delight in the story-telling for its own sake, making new stories from themes that were old in all their lives, giving the ragged fragments of old stories new clothes. These are the best kind of stories for they grow from their own time and place, and none of them written down, for stories – poems too – ring truest not on the page (that deadens their resonances) but on the ear. They are not the stuff of literature's instincts but a core of fact and myth wrapped in inspired improvisation and garnished with Wullie Urquhart's good beer and the land's good whisky.

Natives of the town are called "Sons of the Rock" or "Daughters of the Rock". I think: what a foundation for a life! To be born of the womb of the landscape! Like Adam! It is an idea that excited and impressed me, reinforcing a sense of destination that I had already begun to explore in my mind. The natives, being an unprepossessing tribe, find the whole thing as unremarkable as being born. So much the better. Still, it is a title they use among themselves with a quiet pride, and thoughtlessly overused by the local newspapers.

Rab embodied the idea more than the others. He was hewn from the same dark slab the volcano exhumed. If I have, from time to time, been garbed by the Grace of the Mountain, he was touched by the Grace of the Rock and wore it well. It is a different garb but worn in much the same way – as I now know – and winning the right to wear it is no less arduous. Rab's house was the nearest to the Castle Inn, and when the bar closed and the others would scatter out down the frosted cobbles, he would sometimes climb the narrow and wood-creaking stair to my room where we would talk and drink and watch the mountain skyline from its single window. In these quiet, low-voiced hours I learned about their Place of Strifes. The absence of his friends liberated him strangely. It was as if he were trying to breathe in the mountain wind that had blown me to him. As if alone in my company he were trying to reach beyond the confines of the Rock, the confines of the present. Sometimes I thought he was trying to reach far back and that my company could assist him. Once, after he had left none too steadily (we had been drinking more or less constantly for six hours – 'I'm alright, it's all doonhill fae here,' he assured me as he left), I found him several hours later in the dawn, cold, stiff and staring north from the parapet by the Castle gates. He had turned uphill, not down, not gone home, and he had stood through the late night and the early morning reaching back. When I asked what he was doing there, he turned and smiled and said 'Sobering up' and sauntered off downhill.

But later, at the inn, the thing still chafed at him and it was very late when he climbed to the attic room again. It was clear at once he had borne a burden up my stair.

'Last night,' he said, 'last night…you troubled me with your stories…your mountains, eagles, swans…I think you should know what is at stake here.'

I passed him glass and whisky bottle and water jug. He filled the one from the other two (eagerly, then meagrely), nodded his thanks then stared at the glass in his hand for several minutes without drinking, warring within himself at how and how much to tell me. In the firelight and the narrow pool cast from a single small lamp his face was a mask of shadows. When he spoke he was tentative, unconfident, which was not his way:

'There were times…I was younger…a child…and a younger man than I am now. I was…I don't know…gripped. Some sort of…change would take me…'

He stopped again, helpless for the moment. Had he said more than he intended already? He still stared at the glass in his hand, mesmerised by the firelight's quiet dance there. I sipped from mine then said (tentative myself: I was as uncertain as he was about what should and should not be said and what had been and was to be):

'Change?'

He looked at me directly then gathered himself and at once the shadows were off his face. He said:

'It became a familiar and a loathed thing. A different set of instincts were at work inside me, but they always had to fight their way in to overwhelm my own instincts. They were alien to me. They belonged to someone else I think, from some older far-back folk that were trapped here maybe...some kind of struggle...I don't know. I couldn't understand the demands they made, the voices they spoke in. But the effect was to unsettle my rootedness here. Make me restless. It was like I was being tested; was my loyalty to this place and its people all that it might be? Could I be prised away from my own people, cast free from my Rock? Why should that be, eh? What was the purpose of it all? Whose purpose was it? I don't know. I didn't know then. I don't know now.'

He was quiet again. He drank. The shadows had his face again. The fire spat. I stamped out the small glow on the hearthrug. We both watched its tiny curl of smoke rise and vanish. His eyes looked up. He tried again:

'Y'see, I love this old Rock. I love the way it feels to wake up this close to it.'

He had been holding his glass in both hands, leaning forward. Now he took his right hand from the glass and held it up just in front of his eyes with thumb and forefinger not half an inch apart – that close.

'It's the dark crouching angel on the shoulder of all of us.'

He drank again, appreciatively this time, relishing the sharp warmth on his throat, swallowed.

'I love the way it lords it over the land, the way it feels so massive when you live on it, and makes the mountains small – aye, your beloved bloody mountains. I love its age. I love the way it watches...it has watched for so long. I love its skies, the river that swirls bits of your mountains past its feet, that river that nurtures broods of your swans, man, then sends them away east downstream to the winter firth. Sometimes I walk a mile or two out towards the mountains, then I turn to look back. It is as far as I get, for as soon as I turn, the Rock's before me again, the unconquerable throne of its own landscape. It's like a magnet. No – a lifebelt, it hauls me in safely again.

'There's a tree on the riverbank, an old, old pine, standing on its own, resisted every flood and spate the river ever threw at it. Still there. That's where I stop. It marks my territory. The Carse folk, the old ones anyway, used to call it the Gone Hame Tree...some old story about a herdsman who used to pasture beasts out there long before it was farmed the way it is now. He used to go as far as the tree then let the cattle go on alone because they knew the way from there...the old beasts knew from old summers. So I walk out as far as the Gone Hame Tree, then I turn, herdsman of my own instincts.

'But that change...that thing that used to plague me...it used to drive me further out, up the river or out to the mountains – oh aye, I know these mountains! It even urged me not to turn. But I always turned. Sooner or later I was able to turn. It never managed that kind of hold over me. Sooner or later, the thing was shouted down and beaten.

'And when I turned, I kept one thing in my mind – that old bridge down there. I think you will never understand what it means to be this side of that old bridge. Beyond it...it's too free, too uncontrolled. This side of it, the Rock's side of it, I get my certainties back. That bridge, Neebor, that's the bridge your old wifie was on about! There's your bridge atween landscapes! You're where you're supposed to be alright. But me, I bless that bridge. As long as I'm this side of it, there's no power on earth can budge me.

'But the thing is this...I thought it was all behind me now. I thought I was by with all that. Then last night, after your storying, it was there again. It's been years and years.

When you found me up at the Castle…Jesus, I felt I could have stepped off that Rock and *flown*.

'The thing filled up my heid, filled it with the daft voices and one weird picture…'

The memory of it all crowded in on him, put the shadows back on his face. I asked him quietly:

'The picture. Was it a wing? A white wing?'

He looked up, startled, afraid maybe, the only time I ever saw such an expression on his face. He nodded.

'A white wing,' he said, 'bright as a flame. Nothing else. I couldn't shut the picture of it out of my mind. It burned and burned. A wing like a white flame. Then you turned up and it vanished. Just like that. It hasn't returned. I hope it never does. I want no part of your world, Neebor. It's too exposed. Too unrooted. That umbilical cord that you told us about…the one that ties you to your mountains…it's a long, long cord, man. Look where you are. How tied do you feel now?

'No, don't answer. I know. I know. But I have some advice for you. Don't stay beyond that one winter the old wifie told you to. There are strong pulses here too, and someone like you will feel them and be drawn by them. What do you think has drawn you here already? Lands within lands, you said. Aye, there's lands within lands in every landscape, including this one. You don't have to be a mountain man. Lowlanders are not immune to it either. You can cross the bridge both ways.

'Do what you have to do then go. For your sake as well as ours. Stay too long and you will be torn too, but you will be torn far from your homeland and there will be nothing to cling to. When I was torn, I was on my own ground, well rooted. The lifebelt. Otherwise…'

Rab shrugged into a long silence I felt powerless to break. I waited. A small flame – a blue one, harmless enough – whined in the fire. A bell tower chimed twice. I thought he had finished. He stood to leave, but sat again almost at once. His voice held an accuser's edge:

'You could damage us. Bella feels it already. I can see that. Sammy too. Walter maybe. You won't touch Robert and Chas…they're bedrock. But a place like this needs its own. Only Bella has travelled the way you have. The rest of us are Sons of the Rock. Bella…I can't speak for her. But leave the others, man. Leave the others.'

In the silent hours after Rab left, I made a poem, working it in my own tongue, translating it later:

The Outsider
This welcome is for me
yet these eyes and glad hands
resist more than they embrace.

I sway away from face to face
adrift in seas of smiles.
There are no lifebelts here.

Sometimes I crave a valley
or a street of maternal warmth,
one so founded

on all my certainties
I'd belong wholly. I know
no such place or circumstance,

no congregation of friend
or foe or phantom. Sometimes
I dread such warmth

and feel the cool kin
of swan and mountain wind
belonging enough for the moment.

But what's belonging? Home town?
No. (A shell: I press it to my ear
and cannot hear the sea.)

Childhood fields? No. No longer fields.
Fond forests, shores
and mountains? These seem to suit

me well enough
and I'm more island than most men.
Yet all these see only the Outsider.

They ignore the benevolent instinct
of my passage. So I stand
before the Mountain of Light

to seek its shedding,
but it throws only shadows,
and offering neither more nor less

myself, I take away the same
vague and cold comfort
of my native mountainness.

For the Mountain of Light
is of the same Outsider tribe.
In the starry-sharp December night

the mountain asks the moon
for a share of its radiance. It is
an Outsider's prayer, not knowing

the moon asks much the same of the sun.

Walter had been listening hard. He quoted:

'The cool kin of swan and mountain wind…'

He said "swan" the way I pronounced it myself, the way many northerners do – "swaan".

'Always swaans,' he said, 'and mountains. Ye've tellt wiz about the mountains. Tell wiz about the swaans. Why's it ayeways swaans wi you? What's so special about swaans?'

This was the way these evenings worked. A story or a poem was followed by convivial argument about the performance, or the lack of performance, and the argument often threw up another story. It so closely resembled my own village inn that I marvelled at how it had grown so familiar here in such a short time. So now they had thrown my tradition back at me, and while glasses were filled, pipes stoked and cigerettes lit, Bella dared me a long stare, both troubled and troubling. My own eyes crossed the path of her gaze and in that moment she inadvertently forestalled any possibility of me deftly evading the one question I was quite unprepared to answer. I stayed with her eyes only long enough to read a hesitant sympathy there. I glanced round the table, hoping the moment had passed unnoticed, but of course Rab had caught it, and averted his own eyes the moment I caught them.

So I began, floundering among false starts which puzzled my friends. I was not prone to false starts. But I sensed this was beyond me.

I tried a second, a third time to steer a careful course through the rocks that were suddenly everywhere in my head.

Robert barged in:

'It's simple Sammy. They're big and white and bonnie, they're good to eat, they'll take the finger aff yer hand, they eat the fairmers' grass oo' on the Carse, they shit all owre thur fields then stamp the shit into the ground wi their size twelves. And sometimes they turn into princesses in fairy stories.'

He looked at me grinning.

'That aboo' cover it, Neebor?'

Chas chimed in:

'Yur an idiot, Robert. It's the princesses that turn intae swaans.'

Sammy felt cheated:

'No, there's mair tae this swaan stuff than yur lettin on, eh?'

Then they looked at Sammy and then at me, and it went very quiet. So I tried again.

'There is a tradition, Sammy, among the poets of my country. It is that every poet should carry his own personal legend. Sometimes the legend has a grain of truth to it, sometimes not. Sometimes it will have grown unrecognisable, amended by that poet's followers, ornamented into something he would never be inclined to live up to…but sometimes the plain truth is legend enough.

'So…it was said that a week after I was born, my mother took me to a small lake where the wild swans gather. She was carrying me over stepping stones…a rough causeway crosses a corner of that lake creating a tranquil shallow pool where children swim – when she slipped and fell into the pool. But I fell from her arms the other way into the lake which is deep and wild.

'The swans swimming there were curious and un-threatened by the shape in the water. A big cob swam over, took my shawl in its beak like so much pondweed and pulled me ashore. They said – and this is the legend I bear – that I was baptised by swans.'

Chas spluttered his disbelief, but he was testily silenced by Bella, an uncharacteristic outburst. Frowns then, and embarrassment, a rare and awkward phenomenon in that cameraderie. Chas waded into the silence with a monosyllabic challenge:

'So?'

I shrugged, uncertain where to go from there.

'SO?'

Louder, more querulous.

'Chas, leave it,' said Rab, but Chas was leaving nothing.

'So you are saying – correct me if I'm wrong – that your personal legend is true? I mean, you're a big fella. Say you were – what – eight, nine, ten pounds when you were born? Then you fall into the water and a swan picks you up…this deadweight in waterlogged clothes...in its beak? And that was you baptised. I don't believe a word of it.'

There was no going back now. No way out. No clever, stylish words would ease my situation. I tried to calm that warning fire that had begun to stoke inside me, that white flame I know so well and loathe so well for it signifies only dark anguish. I closed my eyes and put my hands to them for a moment, and as I did so, a voice reached me from far, far back, the thin cry of my mother as she fell.

I said:

'No, I understand your scepticism. This won't get any easier to understand, but I will tell you because I must. You see, I have two fragments of the legend which I can rely on utterly. One is this...'

And I rolled up a sleeve to show, high on my right arm, the mark on my skin where the swan gripped through the shawl.

'As far as you are concerned, it could be anything, a graze, a cut, a birthmark. It is none of these things. It is the imprint of the swan.'

'Aye, aye,' said Chas. 'And the other bit is what...?'

I said bleakly:

'I can remember it.'

The loud and taunting chorus of gasps and scoffs turned every disinterested head in the room on our small group, every unconcerned eye was suddenly rivetted on our fireside table, and suddenly the sound of it all was far, far away like an echo in an empty canyon, and I saw again through closed eyes the lowering bright yellow and black bowsprit of the swan, huge as a sailing ship, as I broke the surface of the lake, saw the unblinking eye as big as a black moon, and knew no fear. Then my head was on the table and my hands were wet with my own tears, and in a sudden and suffocating quiet, I heard them splash twice onto the table.

The arm about my shoulder was Rab's, shielding my distress from the room, angry at the way it had been induced at what he considered to be his hearth. He quietly restored order in the room, called it a night, dispersed his friends saying:

'It's not our way here.'

The others left, confused, apologetic, shaking their heads in blank incomprehension. I didn't want that, but when I lifted my head to urge them back, they were already at the door and only Bella was looking back, unable to make the contact she sought, defeated by unbridgeable distance.

But Rab was controlled, dignified, subtle, purposeful, restoring our mutual confidence carefully until you could almost stand back and admire what he had rebuilt like a sound drystane dyke. Yet in my head a chill wind of unease niggled through a tiny fissure, that small stone Bella had prised loose, so that the thing could not be rebuilt precisely as it had been.

We stood together outside the Castle Inn, Rab and I, the last to leave the bar. The gray town was quiet below us, wrapped in its black night shroud. The air was brittle and pure, borne on the mountain wind. He put a hand on my shoulder.

'All right?'

'All right. Restored. Thanks.'

He nodded, turned to go.

'Rab…'

He turned again.

'Is…was…Bella your woman, in any way?'

'Bella?' He seemed surprised. 'No.'

He made to go, but turned once more and offered:

'I suppose she's here at all because of me, but…oh, some other time, Neebor. Maybe I'll give you a story about it sometime, eh?'

If he did, it would be the first time, for Rab alone among us had contributed not a word to the storying, protesting his chairman's role, his lack of formal education, his this, his that…

I stayed a while by the Castle wall, bearing the brunt of the wind, letting it wash through me, a cleansing, calming air, a healer. My mind was still again when I climbed the stair to my eyrie in the roof of the Rock.

CHAPTER 6

BELLA'S STORY – THE SWAN'S SECRET

ↄ◐◑ↄ

BELLA LEANED FORWARD into the firelight, rested her elbows on the edge of the table, her chin on her hands. She was a striking woman, thick dark hair to her waist, not tall, but a slender neck gave her the grace of tallness. To draw comparison with the neck of a swan in such a woman is one of love poetry's oldest images. Every land that has swans also has its songs that praise swan-beauty in women.

Her locks were like the raven,
Her neck was like the swan,
Her face it was the fairest
That e'er the sun shone on.

She captivated me from the first, as doubtless she captivated all the others. Her voice had the softness of islands. The stories she told wove those strands of nature and supernature which are at the heart of Celtic things; and many of the tales have their counterparts in my own land, for their resonances are the same, the fusion of Celt and Viking.

This was the story she called *The Swan's Secret*:

IT BEGINS again every autumn. A restlessness goes through the wild whooper swans in the north of Iceland like a shiver. They are being summoned.

It is the light that summons them, for their island home is about to lapse into a winter of almost complete darkness. They have only one idea in their heads – south! They drift down the island following routes used by swans for thousands of years. They know its landmarks: the curve of glaciers, the rims of volcanic craters, the white miles of the ice-cap that sits on top of the mountains, and never melts.

At the south shore of the island they pause. Swans gather there from all over the island, answering the summons. It is a loud gathering. The birds converse in brassy voices. News is exchanged, the journey ahead is planned. Excitement fizzes among the groups of birds. Many of them have made the journey before. It makes no difference, they are as excited, as restless, as all the others. But there are, too, the first-timers, the dowdy gray-brown young birds wearing their first clothes. They do not understand, but they hear and they feel the summons, and they have been given many powerful instincts by nature which will serve them well.

Sometimes there are dozens of birds on the gathering grounds, sometimes hundreds, sometimes thousands. Sometimes they leave in a great horde, sometimes in small groups. Sometimes they fly higher than the highest clouds, sometimes no higher than the highest wavetops.

I have said that the swans have only one idea in their heads. It is not quite true. They also carry the secret known only to all swans. But I cannot tell you the secret, at least not yet. The time is not right, nor is this the place. First, the swans must fly from the land of swan-birth to the land of child-death...

...We have an easy crossing, flying at the height of the waves, staying under the wind, landing on the sea. It is almost dark, so we wait for the moon.

All swans love that moon, that huge, silver, night-flying moon. It is the guardian of our secret. If only you could fly with us, you would know that to fly a moonlit ocean as a swan is the most beautiful thing to do in the world.

We fly on again with the moon painting our wings silver and blue, until I see that familiar arc of white sand. Then with a dip of one wing and a scatter of swan words I pull the small skein of my comrades towards a small island off the Scottish coast. And so, for one more autumn, it has begun again.

From here we will scatter across the country, the groups growing smaller, meeting with other groups, moving from place to place, gypsies of the wind and the weather. It will be that way until spring when the old restlessness comes on us again and we answer a new summons: north!

It is not good for you to see what happens next. It has to do with the secret, the secret within all the whooper swans of the north. That secret enslaves us, compels us to heed the summons of autumn and the summons of spring. See what you should not, and you may fall under the secret's enchantment and become swan yourself. It is what happened to me.

A swan drifts away from the others on a quiet bay of the island. It is just before dawn, the quietest, stillest time. Beyond the bay is a small, dark inlet where the water is deep and swift. The swan steps onto a grassy shelf, stands, begins to preen.

Swans preen constantly on land and water. So would you if you had more than thirty thousand feathers to keep in order for flight, for warmth, for waterproofing. And also for the uncovering of the secret. It is that which you should not see.

The swan on the grassy shelf by the inlet preens in a way which is unusual. The beak has begun to work the lowest belly feathers, and slowly draws a straight line right up the breast and neck. The feathers do not lie smoothly in place. Instead a furrow has opened.

The bird stands tall and throws wide its wings, then seems to collapse forward, on to its neck. There is no longer any shape to the swan, only a white cloak of feathers on the grass. Where the swan stood, a child stands, a girl of eight with eyes the blue of island lochans, and long hair the gold of ripened barley. I have flown from the land of my swan-birth to the land of my child-death. I am the girl. I am the secret of the swans.

If you were to look at the house above the inlet you would see a low ruin, roofless, windowless, doorless. It has a floor of nettles. Only sheep go in at the doorway now. There has been no fire in that cold hearth for a hundred and fifty years. But if you were to look at the house through my eyes…

…The roof is thatched with heather. It is pale in the moonlight. A thin smoke comes out of a hole in the roof. The heavy wooden door is never locked. It opens easily on its hinges. The single room is dark and warm and smells of the peat fire. That smell is the happiest smell in the world. That room is the only room I ever knew. Over there, behind that dark red curtain, is the bed where I used to sleep, the only bed I ever knew.

There are two grown-ups asleep in the box bed against the wall…my mother and father. I can cross the floor to the bedside silently. Swan-children make no sound. I do as I do every autumn, I speak the same silent words:

'Death is only a horizon, and a horizon does not exist. It is only the limit of your sight. When I fly a swan, my horizon is much further than yours. I am fine. All is well.'

Of course, they do not hear my words. I kiss the eyes of my sleeping mother, as lightly as if I had used a feather. Of course, she does not feel my kiss. I do not feel sad when I do these things. I am happy to be home again for one night.

I pull the door closed behind me again and step outside into the moonlight. I walk down the old stone path to the croft gate. I pull the gate closed behind me. I run to the shore and I feel the gentle night wind in my hair. Once, long long ago, I ran like this out into an early autumn morning, and there I saw what I should not see – a swan casting off its cloak. A great gust of wind sprang up out of nothing. I was caught off balance and thrown into the inlet. The water was deep and swift. I could not swim.

The following summer, in Iceland, I was born again, as a swan. And now I can swim.

Once more, I run down to the shore. My swan cloak is where I left it. I pull it over me and sleep till dawn. When I awake, I will awake as a swan. So it is, every autumn.

In islands like these, and all down the west coast of Scotland and Ireland (for these are the quiet places, and safe from the eyes of people), swan children go home, but only for one night to speak words of reassurance for those we left behind. In the morning, I know my mother will wake and turn to my father and tell him:

'The dream came last night. Eala is safe.'

My father will nod. He is a quiet, uneasy man. He will put an arm round my mother's shoulders. He will sigh, put on his big boots, and go out into the morning. He will stand for a silent hour, watching the swans swimming out in the bay, wondering. He will tell himself:

'Ah, but she was so young.'

In places like these, the quiet island places, you may still find a few old folk who believe. Never harm a swan, they will tell you, for the swan that flies under the moon is keeping warm the soul of a child who has died. Harm the swan and you harm the child who flies on within.

It is always worth listening to old people who live in the quiet places. They live close to the land. They know things about wild nature that most people can never know. They see things with different eyes, and they feel some things they cannot explain. Whenever you have the chance, listen to them.

Each time I have closed the croft gate at my back I have made a small mark on the gatepost, a scratch with a stone. If you see that gatepost, you might like to count them. I was eight years a child. I have been one hundred and seventy-five years a swan.

CHAPTER 7

'I MUST LEAVE SOMETHING BEHIND...A LINE OF FOOTPRINTS'

∽◌◍◌∾

I FOLLOWED THE river westwards through the flat lands of the Carse of Stirling, turning often to watch the Rock recede into its own landscape, turning again to watch the mountains advance. I walked unmagnetised by that queer power that held Rab in check. I felt no need of lifebelts. I believed then I could take the Carse as I found it, that I could savour its quiet, river-thirled plain, a low-slung land in that landscape of summits.

Familiar sounds on the wind! I walked softly to a field hedge and paused by a gap. Forty or fifty whooper swans were feeding among the stubbles. Others dozed or drank or bathed on the nearby river, taking advantage of a wide and shallow bay where the current was less urgent. The birds' soft contact calls, muted brass, layered the prevailing calm with a lush embellishment. I called out sharply in their swan tongue, heard the anxious response of a sentry bird, saw that single alarm galvanise the relaxed flock into a taut, collective wariness, necks erect, heads high, voices raised. But I called again, the reassurance call, saw them quieten down again, then I could cross their field, as though I were swan myself, for I walked among the cool kin of swan and mountain wind, and in that wild and carefree company I felt strong again and blessed.

The farmer was at the edge of the field, watching. As I approached he said:

'Now if I'd done that, they would have been in the air before I got within fifty yards of them.'

'More like a hundred yards,' I smiled.

'More like. What did you do?'

'We seem to speak the same language. We come from the same part of the world. I have known swans like these since…well, since I was very young. We live close to nature in my homeland. The swans are part of our lives there, and I suppose we are part of theirs. Talking to them never seemed strange.'

'I like that idea,' the farmer said. 'Here, can you do this?'

He put his lips together, and with his tongue and his throat he set up a raucous chattering. At once, there was a chorus of response from a small squadron of magpies. He called again, and from every compass point birds homed in on the tree at his back, guffawing down from the branches. I grinned my admiration.

'No,' I said. 'I certainly cannot. How do you account for that?'

'Same thing. Since I was this high…(he spread a downturned palm by his knee)…You stay in the same place long enough, you become a bit of the nature of the place yourself. That's more or less what you said, isn't it?'

'More, rather than less. It *is* the same thing.'

'I dare say you're the storyteller lad we've been hearing so much about. What on earth brought you here, though, if you're as far from home as the swans are?'

'It's a long story,' I said, 'but what it boils down to is that I suppose the swans brought me here…'

He interrupted:

'Aye, and it's none of my bloody business. Anyway, I can't think of a better reason to travel than to follow the flight path of swans. Aren't they just about the finest things in nature?'

'The finest! I'd say perfection in nature, but I acknowledge a bit of bias.'

'I'd say a lot of bias! If they were perfect they wouldn't trample my field into a mulch.'

'Yet you're happy to have them around. You were just watching them when I came along, after all, not shooting them or scaring them off.'

'Happy, yes. And more than happy. You see that hill across there with the crag and the wee high-up cave and the long gully? I've always thought it looked like a face.

'When I was a boy, I thought it was God's face! My father thought he had spawned an idiot. Maybe he had. But now, every time a small skein of swans flies across, low down, about the line of the larches there, it's like a smile on the face…God smiling! Now what more could a farmer wish for than to have his God smile down on his labours from the hill, eh?'

In my mind as I walked and watched the mountains grow close was a new story I had promised to make for my friends at the inn. It was to be a parable of all my wanderings, a gift in return for friendship, hospitality, warmth. But I hoped it would also be a sown seed, for I had begun to grasp the purpose of what it was the Old Crone would have me learn here. I must leave something behind, a line of footprints in the snow of the world for others to follow.

It was the story that had urged me down from the Rock and out through the Carse towards the mountains. I wanted to revisit the lochan on the Mountain of Light, I wanted to watch golden eagles again, and something the farmer had just said to me had ignited a new idea. This is how I love to make stories, surrounding myself with the very landscapes and creatures I would write about. So I was on the mountain road again, a pilgrim again, and I slipped joyously back into that mountain world which is the womb of my existence, back into that demeanour of mountain-going which was my inheritance before the years of joylessness.

I had not been in the mountains for four months now, the longest absence of my life. Mountains have been this much to me – birthplace, cradle, nursery, garden, school, then all the growing, wandering, climbing, living and writing in their midst, then the long cleansing of the pilgrimage, the despair, the salvation across the old Stirling Bridge. I was taught to think of mountains as the most ancient symbols of the earth, shaped by the very forces that also laid down the oceans and the skies, primitive forces that outlived time itself. Now, walking the calm miles of the Carse, I saw them as if for the first time. When you are born among mountains they are there when you open your eyes for the very first time, you accustom yourself to them as you accustom yourself to your mother's face, you learn their names and their shapes as easily as you learn the names and shapes of other children.

But now, approaching them again after so long and from the broad river valley to the south, they had a new aspect. The flat fields of the Carse began to swell and curve and climb northwards. The land began to harden, the fields grew less fertile, the grazing rougher; the woods dwindled and petered out; the bare places steepened and climbed to mountain skylines. It was a mesmeric transition between landscape extremes and began the moment you crossed that old bridge. The mountains grew as a crop from the fields, and I placed a high value on the Carse-folk's perspective of new-sown mountains rising from the fertility of their fields. The night had draped snow robes far down the slopes and now, in the first light of an unflawed winter morning, they rose into a sky as pale and clear as a writer's empty page.

Such skies!

There were times, especially in the last of the sunset light when the sky grew massive over the westmost mountains sealing off the whole valley and shrinking the skyline summits to a frayed edge of the land. But the dawns following such dusks would peel back the seal and the mountains would have soared again in the night, rising to the sun like opening flowers. It was a sorcerer's landscape.

And from the Carse, the lynchpin of it all was the Mountain of Light. It was from there, surely, that the mountain was named. Whether Mountain of Light or of God, its omnipotency above the farm lands is as unassailable now as it was when the ancients named it. The eyes of the earliest tribes would see how the mountain caught the weather, how it would either steer it clear of them along the summits or hurtle it down on their crops and rude homes. And see how the mountain presides over the warm, benevolent days! Why wouldn't they place their God and their Light there?

I spent a quiet night at Callander, a village that embraces Highland and Lowland at a single crossroads. Its long main street is a spear aimed at the heart of the mountain. It would be a bold place to live, that village.

I was on the road before dawn, the mountain vast and black. I climbed in that deepest shadow and darkest silence that ends all nights on the Highland Edge, respectful as Moses as I climbed.

The summit at sunrise. In its one irrevocable moment, splitting the eastern skyline, convulsive commitment to the forces of light, I felt mountain fires rekindle in me. I knew again the kinship of the mountain midst. I *am* rooted among mountains, as rooted there as the Carse folk are in their river-earth, the sons and daughters on their Rock. Rab was wrong to this extent: mine *is* a flexible realm. My pilgrimage torments had not changed that.

The Mountain of Light threw its shadow far out across the land I would travel in the next few days, looking for eagles, searching for the story. I walked down from the summit to that high shoulder where the Lochan of the Corpse lies, retracing my steps of a few months before after my meeting with Muir the shepherd. The sun touched the lip of a wide corrie below the lochan and lit on a far rock, a conspicuous, irresistible place, Creag na h-Iolaire, the Crag of the Eagle. Its sunlit stance beckoned me. I made my peace there with the Spirit of Eagles. I explained the nature of my presence and my work, guaranteed my conduct in the eagles' domain, all as I was taught as a child. In the eagles' domain, man defers to eagle.

I walked back to the lochan. A skin of ice still clung there, sealing the waters into the cold mountain embrace. I broke the skin and drank.

Then, by way of honouring the renewal-in-landscape ritual of my own country (a reaffirmation of fealty to the Trinity of Spirits – Mountain, Swan and All Nature), I undressed and immersed in the ice-black, peat-dark waters. The cold drew the breath from me in a spasm, which is the right of the wilderness, for it is in wilderness that the breath of all life is stored.

It is by a watersheet such as this, high and aloof and silent in the early morning, and far from the curious gaze of people, that the lost swan-folk of half the world's legends might shed their cloaks of feathers and briefly set aside the enchantment to which they are enslaved, briefly sense their human-ness again. Or…

A soft splash at my back!

Bella at the water's edge. She followed the same ritual, the same words, the undressing, the immersing, gasping at the grip of the water's ice-coldness. Then she crossed the lochan to where I stood. Wordlessly, she laid her neck across mine, began to move in slow sun-wise circles. The pressure of her neck on mine compelled me to turn too, and as we moved our necks shaped and softened and strengthened and entwined in the exquisite and explicit ritual overtures of swans. We rose high on the water, snow breast to snow breast, and nothing remained of our human form.

We linked infinite flexibilities of swans' necks about each other, bowed, parted, entwined again, time after time, clasped again neck-through-neck after each parting, moved to careful rhythms of swan dance. Finally she bowed low across the surface of the water, offering her nape. It was taken. She pulled me down, down so that I was above, submerging her, moving with her until there were only our two swan forms as one, and the ice-black, peat-dark water and the unfathomable depths of the Mountain of Light beneath us. In that embrace we swam deep down through the blackness among the very pulses of the mountain heartbeat. We swam in the first and last embrace of Swans, the embrace of the Mountain, the embrace of All Nature, the Trinity of Spirits honoured. And swan song – the great celebratory anthem of wilderness life – welled between us, a silken binding that held us fast.

The waters lapped clear and cold about our heads. The swan-fires cooled, dowsed. We stood again in the shallows, breathless and cold, joined only by our hands. For our swan-ness was preened away.

That time immediately after the return to the mortal world is awkward and numbing, and a burden to be borne. Only in human form does the changeling know the truth of both worlds, the man's and the swan's. Swans know only the world of swans, the world of wildness. Like all wildness, the concerns of swans are not the concerns of men. There are three concerns of swans, and only three. They are the wellbeing of the tribe; the wellbeing of the land so that it is conducive to the wellbeing of the tribe; and that the land has harmony.

You remember the legend of my birth? It is because of my place in the world of swans that I feel a duty to pass on these concerns, to lay them before men wherever a fertile seedbed might be found. They enshrine wisdoms from which all life can benefit, including the life of men. Yet there are degrees of wisdom and greatness among swans too. All swans defer to those with great wisdom in their midst. So it is with eagles, herons, deer, otters, even wrens, with all the tribes in All Nature.

So I was taught. So I believe.

CHAPTER 8

OF EAGLES, HERONS AND WRENS

⨭⨭⨭

W E LEFT THE mountain shoulder where an old deer
path crosses it, walked down into that folded heartland
of hill country that lies within the radiance of the Mountain
of Light. Walking softly, not speaking, gradually enlivening
in the great quietude of that introspective land, we came on a
strange and impressive place. It lay among many hillsides like a
wide and flat-bottomed cup. Many high-born waters gathered
there, their spirited descents stalled suddenly in the flatness
of the place. The result was a confusion of meanders and
shingles, shallows and pools and pastures. The waters arrived
from every compass point save one – due north. In that
direction flowed the dark and sonorous river born of all that
comingling of streams.

Such places are God-like in their creativity. At the very
least, they are the architects and artists of landscapes. They

gather raw materials from many sources, coalesce all their energies and confusions, give them shape, direction, purpose.

Such places are also like writers and composers, for the way they weave many familiar and unexceptional things (rocks, streams, falls, flowers, birds, mosses, lichens, voles, lizards, deer, otters, foxes, badgers and other thirst-slakers – these are the words and the notes at the mind's disposal) into a new and unique pattern with clear speech and rhythm and purpose. So the newborn river is the book, the symphony. It is the river-purity, the elemental simplicity of that new creation of nature – yet with all its natal strands implied – to which the writer or the composer aspires.

So I had come to watch eagles, so that my story could drink there too. Instincts born of all my mountain travels pointed me at this place. I saw too that the new north-bound river would bear all these mountain waters first north, then east, then south (bathing the feet of the Mountain of Light) then east again until they became that water-snake, the Forth (bathing the feet of the Rock), that Forth across which the old bridge springs. Where better, then, to seek out eagle wisdoms than in the small mountain valleys of all these headwaters?

A great man of eagles once gave me a piece of advice:

'If you want to *see* eagles, you must learn to scan the middle distance.'

It is not as simple as it sounds. It is true you can watch eagles on the eyrie crag or perched for hours on rock or tree, or circling half-a-mile high. But the great man of eagles did not say 'if you want to *watch* eagles…', he said 'if you want to *see* eagles…'

You *see* eagles working their airy alleyways, swerving round a buttress in pursuit of grouse, hugging the contours at zero feet to close in on a mountain hare, striving to gain height with too ambitious a burden of prey slung beneath the powerhouse of their wings, circling to gain a few feet of height with each circle so that a headwall can be crossed. Perhaps it helps if you are born to the mountains like the eagle, as confident in the mountain ways as the eagle, as joyous on the airy stances as the eagle. Even then, your eyes must work along unploughed furrows of air and find focal points there rather than on the hillsides. And even then, there will be whole days when you see nothing of eagles, despite the fact that you are in a place where you know there are eagles to be seen. Sometimes, it seems to me, the eagle decides when it is to be seen and when it is not.

We sat high on the rock-strewn flank of a grassy corrie, Bella facing east, I facing west, both of us with sightlines southwards into corrie and glen, northwards into the long flank of a mountainside drawn taut as a filled mainsail. Settle and still, attune eyes, ears, state of mind. Become a fragment of the landscape. Scan the middle distance…

…A movement after long hours of stillness, but movement now…Bella's touch on my arm and her pointing hand…she had picked the bird, huge and low down and slow, the demeanour of the huntress. What I saw first was the shadow, crossing burn and rock and scree, the low sun projecting a vast shadow-shape there, a black eagle of the gods. The shadow rose from the valley floor to the hillside and climbed. The speed of that climb astounds all eagle watchers every time they see it…a thousand feet in a handful of moments. Then the shadow vanished as the eagle cleared the skyline, dipped a wing, crossed the sky towards us, closed its wings so that it was a tapering missile, and fell towards the pair of us. There is nothing in nature that does not feel a primitive fear crouching beneath a falling eagle. I felt it myself. I was the crouched hare, the ptarmigan, trusting in stillness. Then the bird spread its wings wide, banked into a level circle from which she watched us, appraising our still shapes with fire in her eye and burnished gold on the nape of her neck. Goddess Mother of the Mountain. I lifted an involuntary hand, a gesture of deference. A ripple worked through the wide wingspan and the bird fell away from us, deep into the lower airspaces of the valley, where she was reunited with her shadow. There, too, she began at a new level to furrow the middle distance, goddess no more, but an eagle working for her living again.

For three more days we watched eagles, rising in the dark so that we were in place to see them stir at first light, ghosting back down to camp by the river only after they had roosted. Our evenings were filled with talk of eagles, how, in the years since wolves were lost to these lands, the eagles had become the principal guardians of All Nature there. On our last night, Bella said:

'Strange…we know how swans travel but we do not know the byways eagles travel.'

'What do you mean?'

'It is unsurprising to us that a swan may be able to transform, to become mortal. To know that among those swans that may transform, some manage only a few hours each year, others spend most of their lives as mortals, becoming swan only to cross seas, mountain ranges…'

'Or to mate…the sustaining of the tribe…'

'Or to mate…to know, too, that few swans possess that power, that the wisdom of those few directs and cares for the tribe, the land, the harmony of the land…

'And eagles?' I urged her on.

'Eagles,' she said, 'have such unchallenged pre-eminence in this land…they are such an obvious choice to carry the banner for All Nature. Might there be a few individuals that know a comparable power, share comparable wisdoms?'

'What…they become mortal?' Not even legend – at least none I had ever heard of – suggested the possibility of such a thing.

'I don't think so. They are so wary of people, and with good reason. Only people and hard winters inflict death on eagles. But…perhaps there is a rare bird in which All Nature has placed its trust, perhaps conferred on such a bird the lost wisdom of wolves? Perhaps such a bird knows ways of transforming to move undetected among other influential tribes?'

I considered the idea. I smiled directly into her eyes, remarkable eyes to see such things. I shook my head in admiration. Then, far back in my mind, the idea turned a key in the unwritten story.

We sat quietly for a while, our thoughts sunk deep in the flames of a small campfire. And suddenly our thoughts intertwined like two tendrils of smoke and became one, and we looked up in the same instant.

'My winter here is almost done. The way for me lies north. When the wild swans fly north, shall we go with them?'

She smiled, nodded. Speech was suddenly beyond her. Her captive years on the Rock were freed tears.

Somehow Rab had given her a changed life. There was a hold on her. Perhaps she too felt the power of the Rock. Without the kind of durability my pilgrim years had given me she had become lost to the tribe of swans. But suddenly we both believed that I could free her, that I could win back for her the freedom of enslavement to wilderness. It is the greater freedom, believe me.

'Cross that bridge of landscapes,' the Old One had said.

I have done so. I have been true to the pilgrimage, to the Old One, to all my people, to the tribe of swans, to mountains, to All Nature. There was only the story left, for that was to be my sown seed in the landscape of the Rock, the landscape across the bridge.

The five were in convivial session when we walked into the Castle Inn with the good weariness of the road on us. We had been gone six days, but we were greeted as if it had been six years. We were now two, Bella and I, and they were five again. They knew it, and treated us as if it had always been that way. I sensed the soothing, fear-allaying hand of Rab at work. It showed immeasurable generosity of spirit towards a stranger of only one winter in their midst. It was as though they had invented for themselves the role of collective guardian for the woman among them, and now, at a signal from their unelected leader, relinquished her into my care. Rab was on his feet as soon as we walked in, embraced us both (a show of great affection in one as undemonstrative as a Son of the Rock, but then he alone knew something of the ancient truth that Bella and I shared).

'So, you'll have got the mountains back into your system, eh, the Tall Ones? I suppose that's the way it has to be.'

'I suppose it is, my friend.'

'Yes. Anyway, how's the new story we're all waiting for? Did you find what you were looking for?'

'Yes. We both did.'

Then, for the first time, my eyes linked openly with Rab and Bella and touched and held them across that table in that firelight, and doubt was banished and acceptance was utter.

'Wullie!'

Chas was summoning good ale to slake our road-thirst, whisky to mark the occasion. So we rejoined that great fellowship and became absorbed fragments of the whole again. And I knew that wherever I travelled, it would always be that way.

Walter wanted to know about the story.

'I can tell you this,' I said, 'it's three stories in one, but it still needs a bit of work – I need to skulk among herons a bit, and I need to watch a wren…'

'Bloody herons! Bloody wrens!' sighed Robert. 'Still, I suppose it makes a change fae mair bloody swans. But is there nae *folk* in this bloody story?'

'Aye, good Robert,' Chas endorsed. 'It seems tae me it needs folk, and it needs…Wullie. Wur empty again.'

Walter was a determined ally:

'Thur jist feart they get shown up for no kennin the difference atween a heron an' a wren. Thur's a herony mad wi' shouts in the wuds no a mile fae here, wrens tae. Ah was there yesterday. Ah'll show you the place.'

Walter and I took the road south in the first of the light. I wondered if I might learn about more than herons and wrens from him, wondered if he too would be liberated by distance from his bar room coterie, wondered if he might discuss Rab, for example. He was canny and quiet in the bar, rarely moved to muscle in on the louder talk of the others, given to grinning over his beer a lot. But he was good at the story-telling when the bottle paused before him, funny and observant, sometimes almost instinctively lyrical. Now he guided me companionably through the morning, through the threadbare old village of St Ninians just beyond the town's edge, its old stone hub still clustered close about a square tower.

Walter narrated its history, from the unique point of view of those who have had to pick up its shattered pieces.

'There was this battle up in the Highlands, Culloden, 1746, 16th of April, same birthday as my mother...I never forgave her for that...folk tell you now it was Scotland against England, but it was much worse than that...it was Government troops against Bonnie Prince Charlie's Jacobite rebels tryin to gie us back the Stuart kings. Scot fought against Scot, brother against brother, and it was the beginning of the end. Anytime the English wanti' somethin oo' o' Scotland after that, they kennt how tae get it...jist divide us, Scot against Scot. We fall for it every time. We're a nation o' bar-room scrappers, like nothin' better than tae knock lumps oo' o' each other.'

He gestured at the tower.

'Anyway, the kirk was an ammo dump for the Jacobites and after Culloden some lads, fleein fae the battle on the Prince's advice, blew the whole thing up so that the

Government troops couldnae get their hands on it. And we've been buryin wur dead in the shadow o' the tower ever since, and wur heids in the sand at the same time. One more strife for the old place, eh?'

He shook his head at its pale and peaceful stone. Then he crossed to the base of the tower and patted it. He smiled back at me, a bit self-consciously.

'I like to pay a wee homage to the old anonymous stone-masons who wandered around here through the mediaeval years, the Old Boys, wi' bags o' tools on their shoulders, movin' fae job to job, makin' their wee marks on the stone – see there's yin there – makin' big marks on the landscape. Then some Jacobite nutter comes alang an' blows it up. We get the pieces…'

He shook his head again, and we walked on in silence. I knew then that Rab need have no fears for Walter. He was too much in thrall of the Rock, too sure of his place in the pageant of its strifes. The thought lodged with me: 'That leaves Sammy.'

A stream flows beneath that old churchyard, then emerges above ground into a long, bog-bottomed thicket through which it squirms to a furtive tryst with a darker, more robust water. The squirmer is the unsung Pelstream Burn, the other is a famed page in the country's history, the Bannock Burn. Walter surfaced out of his morose silence and stopped in a small clearing near that confluence of waters.

'There, right there, that's where the first Englishman died, the very first action of the battle, ae June day, 1314, the finest hour o' a' wur strifes. That's a *forge* where you're standing, Neebor, that spot, a forge for a' Scotland. Yet naebody comes here other than me. Naebody. Me? Ah think it's sacred grund. Imagine the hopes and fears in thae fields and bogs that day. The stakes they wur fightin for. Bruce…he wis the king, the great man. A nation builder. Wallace…aye Wallace was the catalyst, a restless spirit, a bit like yerself but Bruce, he picked up the torch, and he kent how to play wi' fire. Ah'm no sure you and Wallace kent whu' you were playin' wi'.'

His stare was so direct at that point it suddenly recalled the eagle glare from above its own shadow. Another silence passed between Walter and I, an opening gulf, but almost at once nature threw a bridge across it: a heron yelped and both our heads turned to follow the sound. Walter beckoned me on to where he parted a small screen of bushes and we could look up to a wood that seethed with the March daftness of a heronry. The wood crackled with the birds' mating season energies. Herons moved between the woodland floor and the canopy with sticks, a cumbersome procession of wings like hoisted sails and legs like trailing stilts. They paused often to mate by the nests, while the wind moved among the branches and the birds and threatened at every gust to topple the whole festival of renewal. The raised voices are neither a sweet nor a soothing symphony to human ears, but then they were devised to seduce heron ears.

And as Walter had promised, there were wrens a-blur on the burn. The cock bird sang and scolded at everything else that moved through his territory, including a heron a hundred times his size. Wrens are nothing daunted.

After about three hours I motioned to Walter that I had seen enough, but his restraining hand and pointing forefinger alerted me to a heron stepping along the bank, closer and closer, until it stood ten feet away, a poised lance to joust with eels. Suddenly a different Walter spoke, almost to himself it seemed:

'He is an old bird, and done.'

A short silence, then:

'He is a gray heron, but there is gray on him too in a way that marks him worn and wild-weary.'

A longer silence.

'Age and the heron are the same colour.'

He looked at me, shrugged and smiled thinly, embarrassed by the other tongue in his head, as embarrassed as I was intrigued.

'What do you mean, Walter?'

He shook his head. I thought the strange voice was gone from him, but then…

'He will reason that this is his last season on the brown burn. By season, he means, thinks of, the mating season, then its aftermath which is all that follows until winter, when the trees grow thin and stand along the banks like herons. Tree and heron are the same rooted shape.'

He spoke now in whispers, for the heron was unnervingly close. The day's first sun struck a dull sheen on the bird's lank cloak. It looked ancient. I asked Walter:

'Have you ever written any of this stuff down? About herons?'

'Me? A *writer!* No me. Ah'm a joiner. But…Ah watch them, and sometimes Ah think Ah'd like to *be* a heron… sometimes, Ah try and put masel inside a heron like this yin, think masel inside its heid. Is it like that wi' you and your swans?'

I shrugged, nodded. But Walter had reverted to his workaday tongue again, and I wanted to lure back the heron-poet. I asked him:

'Do you think he fears death?'

'No.'

'You sound sure.'

He turned his eye from the heron to me, that same unnerving eagle-glare:

'Herons sculpt their lives from three elements. They know of no reason to question a fourth.'

'You think death is just another element to be lived through?'

'Heron death? Yes. Swan death. All nature deaths. I wish I could be sure it was the same for folk, but we've travelled so far from nature.'

He nodded at the heron again. His eye released me.

'But he doesn't welcome death. Folk cast herons in a miserable mould. But listen to that! Look at that!'

He waved his hand at the glad heronry, its sociability, its joy, devoid of death wishes, devoid of death fears, devoted to celebration of nesting, of furthering the cause of the tribe. Another silence from Walter; still the old heron was rooted and close. I sensed Walter's mind at work, struggling between its two realms, as though the thoughts articulated by one had first to be translated laboriously out of the other before they might flow as language. I wondered briefly how many more pent-up poets this land accommodated. Then the barrier fell again.

'He will mind, perhaps, that death will wear him away with its uncompassionate winter, weariness piled on weariness until his old resolve numbs and fails, no dignity in the going. Rather he would have it touch him easy and kind and Christ-like, a summer blessing, not a winter curse. But it never does – winter's what kills herons. And anyway, what right has a heron to choose?'

He shrugged again, rose softly, and we stole away, leaving the heron sunlit and briefly blessed.

'You *should* write these things down, Walter,' I told him as we began the homeward trek.

'No. No me. But you write them into your story if you like them so much. Ah'll no charge. It was you that let them out anyway. You've let lots o' things out for all o' us.'

He had given me the last fragments I needed for the story. I told him I would add his name to Rab's on the dedication page, but he waved the idea away:

'You've dedicated it to Rab and he speaks for all o' us. Ah'm in there already.'

To think I had sought to question Walter about Rab. Now the idea shamed me, and in any case it was clear his loyalty and natural integrity were undefeatable. Instead we wandered companionably home and our speak was all of herons and wrens, and it was Walter I got to know better.

CHAPTER 9

THE WANDERER'S LAST STORY – THE KINGDOM OF THE AGED AND THE WISE

⁂

WE WERE GATHERED. The fire was high. The glasses glittered gold and the bottle stood before Rab. He stood at our loud insistence. He fingered the small, newly-bound story I had given him. It looked too slight for its labours, but then stories always do on the page. He began to read.

The Kingdom of the Aged and Wise. Part one. The Swan Boy.

So that, in the boy's mind, was God's face. That half-mile of jackdaw-tumbled crag, the skyline of his boyhood, that was God's brow. Jackdaws, he reasoned, must be blessed birds to cry their coarse psalms in the furrow of God's brow. He would never lift his airgun to a jackdaw. His father, the farmer, was less than respectful of jackdaws for what he said they did to his new-born lambs, and he was damned if he could see God's face on the hill.

Do you see the dark slash of the gully from the crag to the larches? That was God's nose. No matter that it bisected his brow as well as his face, that was just one of the deepest of his furrows. God of all folk would have deep furrows on his brow.

The gully was the kestrel's. The way he hovered before God's unblinking eye, you knew the kestrel was a blessed bird. The boy would never take the egg of a kestrel. His father was less than respectful of kestrels because they had hooks to their beaks, and nothing with a hook to its beak could have anything to do with the approval of God, and anyway, he was damned if the gully looked like God's nose.

God's eyes? Well his left eye was the high dark oval of the cave, and when the sun was wintering low and his brow glowed yellow, something in that cave – a splash of quartz maybe – shone with an eye-like gleam that stopped the boy's heart. God's right eye was that smooth rock above the scree where the rabbits ran vertically over the razory cobbles as though they were born to it, which of course they were, under the whins, right inside God's heid, the boy thought to himself once. The boy would never set a snare to catch one of God's rabbits. His father was less than respectful of rabbits because…well, because they were rabbits and more akin to Satan's oxters than God's face, and anyway, he was damned if there was a God on the hill, and even if there was, he was damned if He had a cave for one eye and a rock for the other.

That green smirr of larches there, that in the boy's mind was God's mouth, but a mouth so straight and unsmiling and unfrowning you could never tell what God was thinking or whether He was pleased with you or whether he didn't like you staring.

Did he speak? Well, the larches spoke, for the green woodpeckers went in about them and yaffled away like mad things, but the boy knew they couldn't be, for how could madness pucker about the lips of God? So he would never laugh at the madness of yaffles, but rather he tried to understand their puzzling language. His father was less than respectful of the green woodpeckers, thought them "loonies", and birds of ill omen, queer, and more than once he looked sideways at his son, thinking the madness of them was rubbing off. He was damned if there was a God's mouth uttering texts of hill wisdoms among the larches. They were good for a bit of kindling, the larches, but only as a last resort, for larch is a sparky, crackling wood that spits at your hearthrug, and that was the beginning and end of God's munificence on the hill.

So the boy's mind saw his God, and his father, when he bothered to look up at the hill beyond his last field, saw only the hill beyond his last field and wondered what strangeness was at work in his son's head.

He had seen the first stirrings of it that spring when the house martins came in about the farmhouse gables, slinging their own dark arrowheads across the yard, jousting with the droning fly hordes above the summer ponds. He had marked the boy's sudden fascination for the whaups that drenched the fields with their weary old pibrochs and stabbed at the night quiet with yelps; for the rising towers of larksong; for the roller-coaster peewits; for the dark cross of a cruising buzzard.

It was not fitting in a farmer's son, this bird-love, and when the farmer found what he though was the flame that fed the strangeness burning in the boy – a pillow-hidden book by some kilted old fool called Seton Gordon – he decided to fight back with flame of his own. That night the book fed the farmyard bonfire. The boy's cheek burned with salt.

Out in the yard, the farmer felt the wind warm suddenly and shift to the south, saw smoke drift across the face of the hill. He thought uneasily that he could not remember such a wind shift in thirty years of bonfires, but he saw in it only a weather change, perhaps, and his unease was stilled by morning when the wind resumed its westerly groove. He could not know that in those southerly hours, the wind had flicked an ash or two in the face of the hill. It was a sign. A choice had been made here.

The boy's sleepless night paled to a surly trudge through the dawn fields. When he looked up at the hill then, it was to see in the gully and the cave and the rock and the larches the face of his God for the first time. All that spring and summer, the boy was full of his talk about God's face and the birds and animals of the hill. His father saw the bloom of his life's dream – to pass a thriving of his labours on to his only son – wither like a winter thistle. Then came the day of the wild swans.

Winter was beginning to rake over the embers of autumn's last fires, stubbles cracked under first frosts, the gray hill paled with first snows, the burnish of the larches dulled and died out. That winter, when it came, left only wreckage of the bridge built between father and son. The arrival of the whooper swans finished it.

To the boy, the sight of them was the first sip of a new and heady brew of wildness, the first unravelling of the threads that had held his young life together. The swans of his childhod had been pretty, arched swimmers that sat on water. They ate the bread he threw at them and they hissed at the dogs. Mostly they just sat and he never knew why God made a bird with such big wings when all it ever did was sit on water and eat bread. He had yet to learn about the carefully contained wildness of mute swans, but suddenly, in his father's fields, here were swans of a different feather.

They *flew!*

And oh, their wings!

And oh, their voices!

He imagined how each mellow, brassy note began, deep inside the bird, saw it polish and preen and perfect itself as it travelled a mile of dark and echoing corridors inside the swan's body and neck until it suddenly welled into the bird's throat and brimmed from its open mouth out onto the air, into the sunlight, and spilled across the fields as a wild fanfare. Then it caught at his breath, thrummed in his heart, and so filled his head with its insinuating music that he felt he could step at once onto the road to the high, wild places of the Northlands and maybe never return!

He remembered Seton Gordon's cremated pages, and in particular a passage which had so captivated him that he had committed it to memory:

'Shining full on them, the moon lit up their snowy plumage, seeming to impart to it a tinge of warmth in which an artist's eye would have delighted. And indeed, are not the wild

swans things of mysterious beauty in that they are, according to old Highland traditions, often none other than kings' children under enchantment? Have they not been seen on wild and lonely lochs, where they considered themselves secure from human gaze, to put away their plumage and assume human shape in their unsuccessful efforts to free themselves from the spells under which they have been cast?'

The boy used a rise in the ground ahead of him to get closer to the birds, now crouching, now crawling, now squirming so that he ploughed a shallow furrow in the land with his chin, until there were six whooper swans not thirty yards away, heads raising and lowering the yellow and black blaze of their beaks, golden throats muttering muted brass asides, huge black webbed feet pattering and trampling the stubble.

The farmhouse door's slap brought the swans' heads up. The boy's father was on the track to the swans' field, a gun under his arm – some rabbiting ploy – unaware of the boy, unaware of the swans. The swans were aware of the man, but unaware of the boy. The boy, chin-in-the-dirt, was aware of the man and the gun and the swans, and while he could not believe that the gun was for the swans, neither could he be sure it was not. Warn the swans! Launch them before the gun saw them! But keep his own secret too. Life in the farmhouse was difficult enough without his father finding him here, swan-watching.

A stone! The curve and thud of it was enough. Six heads swung. Six trumpets chorused. Six nodded alarm on tall necks. Six necks stretched low and forward. Twelve webs pounded the stubbles. Twelve wings gulped air. The swans flew, and in fleeing the unseen source of the stone, they made straight for the man and the gun. The boy offered a silent "not-that-way" prayer but the birds flew on. They passed not thirty feet over his father's head.

But the man's stride never faltered. His head-down father had not even noticed the swans! Could any man, any man anywhere, any man in all the history of all the farming folk who ever lived and stamped over all the stubble fields in the whole world be quite so tragically *dull?* Not to notice the flight of swans – what a curse on the mind of a man!

The swans banked and slipped into a gentle crescent formation, so that as they crossed the boy's God-face hillside, they put the white curve of their flight across the larches. The boy gasped. GOD SMILED.

The boy forgot himself. He stood up and yelled:

'Look Faither! God smiles!'

The man looked up at that. He saw the boy, pointing. He saw the hill, the flying swans, understood none of it. But he decided in that moment to wipe that God and the smile of him off the face of the hill forever; put the torment of it out of his son's head once and for all. The gun barked. The swans fell and fell. The boy ran and ran and ran and the rain of his tears drenched his fallen world.

There was a late afternoon flaring of white sunlight. The farmer saw his son suddenly, standing on the trunk of a fallen oak near the yard. The low sun at his back turned the boy to black stone. The voice when it spoke was not the voice of the boy his father knew. The words were not the words his son might have spoken; this was no farmer's son. The boy said:

'It is not for men to choose the guardians of the land. There are forces beyond men, beyond land. There are lands within lands. It is for the force of the wilds, All Nature, to choose. It is the right of the wilds to plough or scorn the plough. It is the right of the wilds to determine a good lambing or a bad, a gold harvest or a black. The wilds judge according to how men care for the land and its creatures.'

His father heard his son, doubting his own eyes and ears, and wrestled briefly with the idea that he was asleep and dreaming. The voice softened and the power of it chilled with its softness:

'Only the wilds have the right to fell a swan. You do not have that right. The wilds now assert that right over you. The wilds choose a new guardian. They choose me.'

The boy leaped down from the slain tree. Sunlight blazed in the farmer's eyes, so that when he recovered from its dazzle, his son, or whatever it was that had just visited him, was running past the crumpled swans, halfway to the hill by now.

Incomprehension turned to anger in the man. He lumbered a token pursuit, panting oaths, but the corpses of the swans halted him, silenced the flow of his word-torrents. For they were not swans at all but ewes, six of his own best ewes, each with his own gunshot wounds reddening their fleeces. Six jackdaws flew up at his approach. There was not an eye left in the six warm sheep heads.

A hill shepherd found the boy's body, brought it down, havering about seeing the boy by the hill loch covered in what looked like feathers, swan feathers he said, 'then he just walked oot an' droont issel'. But you could see by looking at the boy's drowned face that he was no more swan than you or the next man. And what would the boy be doing smothering himself in feathers, his father demanded? But dark clouds of doubt swathed him and he carried his son home, limp and lifelesss and cold.

That night, seven whooper swans boarded a quiet south wind over the high hill loch, but by morning, the wind was back in its westerly groove.

Rab paused and poured.

He took a long, thoughtful swig from his glass, looked at me, shook his head, looked back at the new page he had turned. He read the first few lines silently, nodded at Walter, cleared his throat, began again.

Part two. The Kingdom. The heron was an old bird, and done. He was a gray heron but there was gray on him too that marked him worn and wild-weary. Age and the heron are the same colour. This, he reasoned, would be his last summer on the Brown Burn, these his last summer suns to put a full sheen on the lank gray of his cloak, this the last season of warmth to soothe his old bones and burnish his blunted lance, this the last alder-darkened pool to shade and cool him.

Soon enough the leaves would fall, the sun arc low and pale across familiar island silhouettes beyond where mountain and ocean waters mingled, the sweet and the salt. Then the trees would stand around the winter burns like herons. Tree and heron are the same rooted shape.

The heron did not fear death. Herons sculpt their lives from three elements. They know no reason to fear a fourth. Death for a heron is one more element to be lived through. Yet neither does the heron welcome death. Men cast herons in a miserable mould, what with a hunched melancholy and a witch's stab, but the sociabilities and festivities of the heronry confound the mould-makers. So there was no death wish on the Brown Burn. The white life-gleam still glowed in the old heron.

The final gray finger would beckon and touch in the coldest, hardest days. He minded, perhaps, that its way would be to wear him out with uncompassionate winter, weariness piled on weariness, until his old and numbed resolve failed, no dignity in the going. Rather it should touch him kindly, on a day such as this by pools such as these, a summer blessing rather than a winter curse. But what right had a heron to choose?

It had been a placid year. The heron had stayed away from the heronry on the sky edge of the old pinewood, spared himself its tantrums. Suddenly these seemed the ways of other birds. He had watched for a while its rituals of stretching, snapping, shouting, but its first February day was a cold, unkindling moment.

So he set himself apart, put the peninsula between him and the pinewood, held hard to the mountainside, and fished the Brown Burn. He felt easy with his oneness. Oneness and the old heron are the same frame of mind.

The Brown Burn was shaded by groves of alder, willow, hazel, birch, rowan, aspen. Its source lay twenty heron minutes inland from the sea. It was a dark water that paled only to leap a mossy fall, only to dislodge a dipper so that the bird's breast flowed through the water beneath it as it flew. It was really three burns, triplets of the same stony womb, a high lochan stitched like a sequin to the mountain's seaward shoulder.

Two of the burns, the Rough and the Red, leapt into life like frogs freed from tadpole shackles. They sprang icily into the shadow of a great crag to entwine amid the first of the birches beneath a fox cairn. The third burn, the Yellow, followed the droop of the hill shoulder, sprawled down the crook of its arm, and emerged from its gully to snake back to a shadowy tryst with the others of its spawning ground. Fifty feet below the fox cairn, then, the Brown Burn gathered up its threefold life and turned for the coast.

It was a benevolent water for a heron-in-exile. Eels crammed their migrations through its narrows and there were fish enough in the pools and shallows of the burn and its small bay to satisfy the heron, but never such a glut that his hunting instinct would grow dull.

Old he might be, and slower, but he was also unique among herons. For with his age grew wisdoms. It would occur to him when he used a new skill to thwart fish cunning or snatch a sprinting vole or a bouncing frog that he had grown strangely wise, wiser than any heron he had ever encountered. For example, he had begun to see the land and its wildness in shapes that went beyond herons. Although he had never known such a notion before, he began to explore it with flights of his mind, suspecting a purpose without knowing what that purpose might be.

He had also grown older than any heron he knew of, and although he had travelled little inland, other wandering herons he encountered had begun to confer on him a formal respect which perplexed him. It is rare in the wilds to treat age with reverence. It is the tribe, not the individual, that matters, and the tribe is sustained by the young and healthy, not the old and weary. The old master stag on the mountain is driven from his harem by a younger usurper to thole a gray year in the Corrie of the Exile. There are many parallels.

The heron had begun to wind and weave the threads of these thoughts through his long and solitary days on the Brown Burn. It occurred to him too how little he was disturbed, as though a space had been made in his life for the weaving. What he wove was a tapestry of the mind, the theme of which was all birds and their ways and their wildness. At first it seemed there was nothing more than random snatches of thought, straws on the west wind, but slowly through the summer days and dusks, a pattern, a design, a meaning began to emerge. Soon the thinking consumed him. The tapestry that had begun to evolve amazed him with its flawlessness, its strength, its purity. He stood through one blue afternoon, its pastel evening and lingering dusk, scrutinising every thread, rehearsing the weave of this thread into that. Thread after thread began to slip surely into place, as surely as waifs of grass stitch the meadow pipit's nest. It was sound.

All this the heron pondered without conceit, and with the same detached analysis of his new creation, he pondered its usefulness. He was fairly sure no other heron could penetrate its weave or grasp the breadth of its embrace, but he was sure too that if he understood it, perhaps there were other birds – a very few other birds – which might also understand.

The heron began to consider his fellows on the Brown Burn. He was unpersuaded by the kingfisher – too flash, and he distrusted any bird that burrowed. The dipper – too enslaved to watercourses, too inflexible in its ways, too weird in its underwatering. Wagtail – too fidgety for contemplation. Swallow – too thirled to the sun. Then he thought of the wren.

At first glance the wren seemed the least promising of all, but because he could not pin down immediately why it seemed so unpromising, the heron thought about the wren again. He realised that while the unpractised eye might see the flat-out impatience of wrens to be at odds with heron stealth, just as his was a patience to survive, so the wren's was an impatience to survive. Wrens knew winter's assassins better than most, crammed themselves into riverbank crannies ten at a time for winter-thwarting warmth. Warmth! In a wren's wrap! The heron had single feathers that could wrap a wren. Yet here about his feet and legs was a survivor of three winters to his certain knowledge, and which, in selfless pursuit of the wellbeing of its tribe, had built four nests and won three mates and furnished them with all they required, flew tirelessly and fetched and carried at all their becks and calls.

The heron was impressed by the sites of two of the wren's nests. That last winter had felled an old pine. It had been a heron landmark, a staunch beckoner for generations of the coast's herons to the shelter of the Brown Burn. But now it lay where it fell. Impotent claws of roots raked the air a dozen feet above the bank. In the highest clasp of the roots the wren had built, twice. The heron saw small life bud and blossom in the corpse of the pine and saw in that gesture the work of a wild justice.

Wild justice impressed the heron. It was the only law by which he lived, by which he would die. It was all he believed in. So at dusk, the heron stepped up to the wren's roost. And while the wren rested and stored energy for the next day's foragings, the heron revealed what it was he had woven. It was a crude communication in terms of the sophisticated language of men, but through pose, gesture, claw scrapings and all the articulations and expressionful repertoire of the heron's neck and head, he found a language fit for what he had to communicate.

The wren heard, saw insights, recognised reason. And then the wren sensed that everything that had ever been, everywhere that had ever been, all things, all places, all birds, were bonded, directed by and to this single thing, this single place, this singular heron. Then the old heron was still.

Snipe drummed in the dawn. Dippers sang of all mornings and all seasons, which is their way. Owls quietened and found cool, secret places to stand away the day, which is their way. The burn was suddenly louder in the heron's silence. Its different waters lapped and overlapped, dripped and splashed, raced and dawdled, sank and swam. All these waters spoke in one unconfused Babel which was the burn's voice.

The heron wanted a judgement. The wren gave it.

This must have wings, was the wren's judgement. At that, the wren sat back, more in the manner of eagles than wrens, raised the feathers of its tiny nape (another eagle gesture) and in that uncanny attitude pronounced that the heron's tapestry should be spread 'in the kingdom'. The heron was puzzled.

- In the kingdom?
- Yes. And its wisdoms are great, but they have been set only in the context of all birds. It is too narrow.

- Narrow? All birds – too narrow? What is wider than all birds?
- All creatures. All places where creatures flourish. All Nature.
- But the kingdom – what kingdom?
- The Kingdom of the Aged and Wise.
- Where?
- Beyond the scope of mere wrens.

The wren had lost its eagle pose and was wren again, deferential and quiet. The change was marked by the heron. The meeting had scattered new threads about his feet. These must be set against the taspestry to see how they might be woven in. He flew off with the sunrise.

The heron's flight had become a daily ritual, threading the burn's landmarks in ascending order – rowan pool, dark shallows, waterfall, high birch – then peeling off while attuning his ear to the slower speech of the Yellow Burn, turning again for the notch in the hill skyline. Beyond that, on a sunny shelf, was the pool. But such was the grasp of the night's thoughts on his mind, that on this of all days the heron's journey faltered. He never reached the pool. He drifted, unnoticing, on a south wind, climbed too high, overshot the notch, and when a casual glance reassured with the sight of a small watersheet another mile to the east, he simply set the droop of his wings towards it. On he flew, oblivious to destiny's deception. It was only as the heron contemplated landing that realisation asserted itself. The landscape was quite devoid of familiar landmarks. The casually spied lochan proved to be no such thing, but a small plateau of grass thrust up from the body of the hills, a volcanic fluke. He had been deceived by the low sun illuminating the dew.

Suspicion dawned. He of all birds had never been so deceived. The deception was hardly consistent with his new-found wisdom!

Then the wisdom prevailed again. This, he told himself, has purpose. There is undeclared intent here. There is unspecified presence. There is unspoken command.

The heron reconstructed the journey in his mind and realised he had been deflected by a south wind, and judged that a fit command.

The plateau was host to a gathering. All manner of birds, all manner of creatures, thronged the place. Others still homed in on its green beacon. As the heron alighted, a mole ascended and sat blinking at the bird's huge foot. Every creature had been as deceived as the heron, and all were convinced by the nature of the command. All bore a kind of authority, all were uncommonly eloquent and dignified, the stamp (it seemed to the heron) of the aged and wise, and as the notion occurred to him he remembered the wren.

A shadow crossed the gathering and stilled it. The vastness of its passing, the rasping air of its wingbeats, were all they needed to know to brand it "eagle". Many of them had cause to know that silhouette, to fear it. Many had survived to a great age only by learning to avoid or outwit such a shadow. The great bird perched, pulled its vast feathers close like a monarch adjusting a robe. She was Goddess Mother of the Mountain. She addressed the gathering in that tongue that unites all creatures, the breath of the south wind. It does not translate well, of course, for although it may appear shallow in that quality called literature, it communicates in depths of the spirit long unexplored by humankind. But this might serve as a reasonable account of those aspects of its language which we might understand:

You are summoned to the Kingdom of the Aged and Wise.

You are the summits of knowledge piled from gray dust, hewn from gray rock, shaped by the sacred south wind and the accumulated generations of all your tribes.

Your very wildness is at risk.

I have been among you in many guises, travelling far.

I am Goddess Mother of the Mountain, and the Spirit of Wilderness. I grieve for my realm.

Wilderness is torn and tarnished.

You are the last hope for Wilderness. There are great wisdoms among you. But these wisdoms you store up as the jay harbours acorns or the squirrel pine cones. Now you must breach your store. Apply your wisdoms beyond the needs of self.

Scatter the seeds of your knowledge.

Foster territory. Reclaim old lands you have yielded in the past. Dare new lands.

Put your wildness beyond everything.

Work together.

A heron of the west bears a tapestry woven from the threads of life of all creatures. It is a wondrous work. He will share it. Examine it. Listen to it. Learn from it. Offer and receive wisdoms.

Take heed. It is winter for Wilderness.

Take heart. Give Wilderness a new spring.

A place has been set aside to the east, beyond the mountain edge, where an imperishable rock is guarded by the river-snake.

The new wisdoms can root there. A beginning will be made there.

An otter asked how all this might be done "in the face of the stain-maker", by which he meant man and his ability to stain the land any colour he chose.

The south wind has chosen a new swan.

Here was news! The gathering whispered, the way a soft wind enlivens a grove of aspens.

There is a child of the Kingdom. He is of this place. He will be an instrument of the heron's wisdom.

The otter asked how the child was chosen.

His God was a hillside. He sided not with the stain-maker but with the swan.

Rab paused again, poured and drank.

A log spat in the silence.

'Larch, probably,' said Robert, who approved of all silence-breakers.

Rab announced:

Part three. The Tapestry. The boy's father, the farmer, died the death of a broken and tormented man. By then, his farm had withered and wildered while the dark face of the hill glowered down. People on the Carse spoke of sorcery, witchery, and worse, and stayed away from the place. Tilled ground reverted back to nature, buildings to rubble. The river, so long held in check by agriculture, gnawed at its own banks and reverted to its ancient course. Tidal bores raged into the old fields, and with every flood, a little more of the old order was swept away. People gave the place a bad name. Haunted. Damned. Cursed. Neighbouring property became worthless. Farm folk fled its scent of decay and doom. Landowners cut their losses, retreated to less troublesome lands in the south. As they retreated, wilderness advanced. The river resettled, alders flourished along the new banks, birches, pines and oaks swarmed across the old fields. Stoats and weasels and small birds thrived in a new and jungly undergrowth amid the resurrected woods. Kingfishers strung jewels through the low branches on the banks. Barn owls nested in a broken chimney, flew in and out over the fallen lintel. Kites and harriers quartered the land unmolested. Merlins scudded across advancing moors. Marshes long since drained responded to the urgings of the redefined river and recreated themselves. Wildfowl and wetland burgeoned.

The winter waters echoed with the exuberant bands of whooper swans.

Otters came. They were long thirled to the mountain and island places of the north and west, but now they scented along instinctive paths and found the ancient traces of forebears. They found the rivers clean, waters reedy, banks woody, the fishing good, the stench of man stale.

They were led by a big gray-muzzled dog, a chieftain of his tribe. He found in the new place two of the oldest, grayest birds he had ever met, one a heron, one a whooper swan. He was familiar enough with the autumn and spring arrival and departure of these migrant swans, but here, when the swans were accustomed to heel north in the spring, some had stayed and nested. Because he knew the needs of such swans, he knew for sure now that the land was changing.

One of the swans bore great age with such dignity that he commanded the respect of all birds, all creatures, save the old heron, to which the swan seemed to defer, although he was treated as an equal in return. The otter, symbol of the most sensitive of all nature's tribes in that land, sensed a pivotal presence about these birds, sensed that their age and wisdom were the loom on which all this wild finery was woven and stained. The stain-maker had fled, and now the dyes and tinctures of Wilderness spilled from the palette of All Nature. The brightest dye of all was hope.

Wilderness was fighting back, like a badger on a terrier, winning back with every blow a wood, a fold in the hills, a square mile of marsh. Its weaving fascinated the otter, but something eluded him. How it worked he could fathom. How and why it had begun he could not. So he took his tribal curiosity to the same still pool where the swan and the heron were to be found in the June dusk. He told them all he had found, and none of what he guessed. Heron and swan saw a kindred creature. The heron said they had waited, worked beyond time, for a meeting such as this. The swan said that when otters of all creatures had found a way back, there would be a watershed. Their talk flowed through the night, until, in the dawn, there was nothing they could add to the otter's understanding.

A great shadow turned all their heads. The eagle.

Heron and eagle passed a greeting with their eyes. The eagle then addressed the three creatures which had been touched by the Spirit of the Wilderness.

A tide has turned here. The Kingdom is well served.

Swan – your song is sung. Cast your cloak. Walk as you once walked. Walk for Wilderness, for All Nature.

Otter – the stain-maker may not always stay away. You who shun him most are best served to foster Wilderness. Dress new lands in the tapestry.

Heron – shed your burden. Your work is done. You are honoured among all birds, all creatures, All Nature. The Kingdom is yours.

On the Brown Burn, life slipped away from an old heron where he roosted by a still and dark summer pool. Death touched him kindly and warm, a summer blessing.

On the Carse, a young man walked softly. He came on the ruin of a farm, worked old stones and timbers into a small cottage, low to the ground. He tended not crops but the wildness of the land, lived closer to the animal state than any man had done there before. He called the place Strivelin to mark the last great strife of that place. He had an uncommon way with swans.

CHAPTER 10

'THE AGE AND WISDOM YOU ACQUIRE IN ONE LIFE ACCUMULATES AND YOU ARE REBORN IN THE NEXT ALREADY WISE'

✑✑✑

RAB NODDED and smiled at me, poured one more drink and sat down gratefully. Everyone had opinions about it all at once and an hour of robust argument slipped past. Then Sammy asked:

'See this Kingdom – your country, eh? Or is it this yin? Or someplace invented?'

'It's everyone's country, Sammy. Yours and mine, but I suppose it was more yours than mine for the purpose of the story. You see, in my country there is an ancient belief in eternal renewal for all life. So the age and wisdom you acquire in one life accumulates and you are reborn in the next, already wise.'

Robert heaved in his scepticism:

'That way you can remember a swan nippin' your airm when you were a week old?'

'Good Robert,' said Chas, who was just as unnerved by my talk of swans and their powers, and for as long as swans have turned the heads of men and fuelled their flights of fancy and their darkest dreams, there have been countless rooted folk like Robert and Chas who are just as unmoved by that mesmerism of swan, cold to it.

I shrugged. It is an insuperable force, that coldness, but then there was a touch on my shoulder. I lifted my eyes and found Bella's, that same look with which she had tried to reach me once before, but this time without the intervening distance. I drew deeply on the surge of confidence she had somehow just put at my disposal.

'Don't be overawed by these claims I make for my own people,' I said. 'They are not extravagant claims. It is not even an extravagant wisdom I'm talking about. In many ways it is limited. There is much about the world that passes by a people so locked into its own mountain regime, much about which we are ignorant, but the wisdom we do have is a great strength to us because it stems from a handful of simple truths. It doesn't make me better than you, Robert, just different. And not so different that I cannot spend these winter months at this fire and admire – even envy at times – your rootedness in this place. Sons of the Rock! I marvel at the very sound of the words.

'But…take this pilgrimage of mine. It has been twenty years among the mountain lands north of this Rock of yours. Twenty years, but it amounts to nothing more than the search for a single truth – the worth of Wilderness. I think now that I have found it, and that what I have found is unshakeable, unflawed, perfect.

'Simply, my truth is that Wilderness is the only perfection, the only purity. It is aware of its own worth, and because of that it will defend itself. The resistance will stem from within, as it must. Nature must emerge in time and reclaim that which was Wilderness, or at least reclaim enough of it to ensure the survival of the regenerating heartland of Wilderness – the mountains.

'Then it will be we who must readjust, for the regime of Wilderness will insist on laws not of our making. That will be the last test for men, and it will determine *our* right to survive. For Wilderness *will* renew.'

'Good neebor,' said Chas, but his face was a blank page and his eyes were on the floor.

So I looked long and quiet at Rab and Bella and the others, saw their firelight faces and remembered. Remembered how it was, remembered all that had been and gone. Now that it was all but over I felt strangely adrift from the table where we all sat and I seemed to see that fireside group as from a great distance. The talk was relaxed and good humoured, but I heard it as far murmurs, like the sea in a shell at my ear. I never admired and envied them more than I did that night, their Rock-sureness, their loose closeness, and briefly I considered stepping quietly away from it all there and then, leaving them all there and then, the circle intact as I had found it. But it had all gone too far to leave things as I had found them. One by one I separated their faces from the circle of bonhomie and remembered…

…Wee Sammy, the futret, the weasel-curious, the thinker; Walter the sometimes-poet, the raconteur and the clam; drouthy Chas, the sceptic, blunt, open, as honest as he was undevious; Robert, his big-boned ally, the silence-shunner who had seen through more than he cared to admit, who wore the patience of his Rock; Rab, who held the cameraderie in check and intact, whose open face concealed a great darkness…wherever I was bound now, a part of them all and a fragment of their Rock would accompany me; Bella, who was still a part of the circle but now a part of me too, who I had somehow freed so that swans might fly freer, who would fly now as my shadow, and I as hers. I looked on them all and remembered…

…remembered how it had been through all my days and nights on the Rock and its edge-of-the-mountains land…

…remembered the sky-fired mountains over my shoulder that first night I crossed the old bridge and climbed the Rock, wondering…

…remembered the same mountains over my shoulder that last night I crossed the old bridge and climbed the Rock with Bella beside me, the wondering done.

I spent the last night of that winter on the Rock alone in the attic room of the Castle Inn, unsleeping, at ease, watching the Mountain of Light toss the moon from silhouette shoulder to shoulder like a slow juggler, watching it blacken, then watching it pale in the dawn. My mind washed over the handful of answers I had gleaned from the thousands of questions that punctuated the pilgrim years. It is a restless mind that pursues any great truth. Now there was a year left for me to reclaim my poet's inheritance in the mountain valley of my birth. It would be time enough with swan wings to lend flight to the journey.

A tap at the door. Bella, eager for the journeying.

There were no farewells left to say. We stepped out into the quiet morning of the Rock, walking softly downhill from the castle towards the bridge. It is always good when a long journey begins with a descent.

We paused and turned when we reached the old Stirling Bridge, irresistible hail and farewell to the town. We saw the small gathering of five high on the Rock, waving. We turned a second time after another mile, but by then the watchers had folded back into the resolute mask of the Place of Strifes. I imagined them trudging up to the inn, heaving open the old door of the back bar, glancing at the blaze in the hearth, summoning Wullie Urquhart to attend to their throats. We turned our backs again and the Rock was behind us forever, but in our minds it would be before us forever.

Far up the lochside that darkens in the shadow of the Mountain of Light, we called a halt in the early evening. Bella said:

'I have still a lot to tell you, a bit at a time, and in my own time, but it began here.'

It was the narrowest stretch of the loch where we sat, the mountain huge and dark above us. Bella handed me a small sheaf of papers, bound in much the same way as the story I had presented to Rab. She said:

'Rab gave me this last night for you. It's the story he promised you.'

The first of no more than a dozen handwritten pages bore the dedication:

'To the Tall One who restored some, but not all my faith in the tribe of the wild swans, and all my faith in the tribe of Wanderers. Yours is the kingdom.'

The second page bore the two-word title of his story, that name by which the wild whooper swans are known to science – *Cygnus cygnus.*

CHAPTER 11

RAB'S STORY FOR THE WANDERER – *CYGNUS CYGNUS*

⤶꙰꙰⤷

TWELVE SWANS (I remember it was twelve) flew through the thin dawn mist. I am the boatman on that water. The girl and the old man awaited me on the shore. New snow, frail as thistledown, was on the air. The loch wore a sheen, the unfathomable gray-white of pearls. The mountains pressed in darkly on the waist of the loch, imponderable walls at that early hour, pale only where old snow lay on their black crags and scattered woods. Cloud smothered summits and shoulders.

All that (the first flurries, the mist, the wan loch, the shrouded mountains) were as an off-white canvas such as an artist might prepare to lend his centrepiece its sharpest focus. The bright gouache of the swans graced it.

They flew as an arrowhead, six and five behind the leader, so that one bird overlapped at the rear of the formation, an unbalanced skein, an ill omen.

I remember the girl's words when she saw the swans 'Perfect!'

And her voice was a belled note adrift on that furlong of water that lay between us. Her eyes were on the swans, her hands clutching at the old man's arm. She was intent on immortalising the moment:

'A painting! No…a poem! Oh, aren't they fine!'

These words swam across to me, excited highlights of her conversation. Indeed, why would she not be enchanted for the sight and the sound of the birds cut a handsome, silken image. The water reflected their flight, but dully, imperfectly, as though through a flimsy screen. The snow thickened suddenly to a limp gray veil as the swans cleaved an irresistible headway.

'A song of swans! An aria!' Her enchantment took wing while I rowed closer, bowed by my boatman's burden. I could see them clearly now when I turned my head. They sat close on a flat rock on the shingle shore. She turned to him. She would see the snow feather his white hair. He did not return her gaze but looked after the swans. With his head still turned from her, he spoke, a deep and certain voice:

'A painting? No. Let your mind frame it. Let time be its locket. One day you will find another winter water, another new snow, another skein of swans, and you will have this moment with you, within you, and remember. A painting, a poem, a song…all these would be elsewhere, fading on a wall in a far town house, locked in a dusty drawer, strangled on the cracked lips of an unsung score. Rather look. Listen. Catch hold of the moment, then, let it go. That way you will recall not just the flight but the freedom of the flight.'

For some moments after the trailing twelfth swan had vanished into the snow, the soft brassy chatter of the skein still drifted over the water as a wake that eddied out to the mountain walls then rippled back, rippled back, so that it seemed to rock my boat as I rowed.

He spoke again:

'*Cygnus cygnus.* Swan swan is the meaning of the name. Think of them that way, for these are all that swans should be, perfect creations. All other swans but these are flawed. Their imperfections displease me.'

By now she would be quite entranced. It is usual. The man's words and the flight of the swans would be a whirlwind in her head. She would already have begun to recreate that flight again and again so that she desired flight more than life itself, which is what he would presently ask of her. She would believe in the perfection. She would love him for his talk. That, too, is normal.

She would try, in vain, to unravel his mind. How did it sing to wild rhythms such as these? How compose its fey beauties? How translate nature's lyric? But she would not unravel it for she was still mortal, still earthbound, whereas he had flown beyond. I could see swanflight in his eyes.

She shivered suddenly. She gave him half a glance, but now she found his smile full on her, the final enchantment.

'Come,' he said. 'We will go. We will follow the swans.'

At that he stepped past my boat and walked out into the water (for it is not my purpose to ferry them from shore to shore, that is not why the boatman is summoned). When next he spoke his voice was the belling brass of the whooper swan. She saw him put on swan shape and stepped after him, enslaved and unafraid, into the deep water. She followed until she drowned. It is not given to the boatman to prevent such things.

I found her where I knew I would, in the reeds. The river that runs deep and dark and unseen through the heart of the loch had ferried her there. She was a great beauty, even after her death, but then they always are, one way or another.

I rowed her body to the village at the head of the loch. If the villagers ever wonder why it is that I always find the corpses, they keep their questions to themselves. As I rowed, I heard the swans again, lifted my face to them and cried out. It is only in my most anguished moments now that my voice still emerges brassy and swanlike. Fourteen swans (I remember it was fourteen). They flew as an arrowhead, seven and six behind the leader so that one bird overlapped at the rear of the formation, an unbalanced skein, an ill omen.

And I have seen the flaw in the perfect creation.

And I have turned my back on the ways of swans. I have my loch and mountain beauties, I have my immortality which they cannot reclaim, but they do not forgive, and I am shackled to the burden of my trade.

And I am the Boatman of Swans.

And I ply this water forever.

CHAPTER 12

'WE HAVE CONSPIRED TO GUIDE
YOU IN SWANFLIGHT'

❧

THE BOATMAN is the outcast among the tribe of all swans. He has broken faith with the wildness of swans in some way. His penance is that he is at the command of swans forever, or until he renders them some service that absolves him. So I had been taught, but there are many places where the paths of truth and fable cross among the myriad ways of swans, and truth grows a confused plumage. Here was one such crossroads.

And here was a deep glimpse into the darkness that clouded Rab's open face from time to time. I read his story again and heard it in his voice, and for a moment I was so persuaded by it that I wondered if this explained his hold over Bella: that he had pulled her from the water an ailing swan and revived her a maiden (for that too is said to be a duty of the boatman)?

Bella saw my anguish and giggled mischievously. I realised then that it was the first time I had heard her do that and I laughed with her for the liberation of that imprisoned sound, and at my own foolishness. But then Bella said:

'Rab will not have told you this. He is – was – a bard, a very great poet – for a Lowlander! But he is also of the tribe of mute swans. Men have puzzled over its name in English for centuries here. Who first named it, and why should a bird of so many sounds be called mute? There are, of course, many absurd theories, but the truth is the boatman of the swan tribe is compelled to silence as well as obedience.'

'So in accordance with his tradition, a written story rather than a spoken one…but how much is story, Bella, and how much is more than story?' I asked.

'*You* ask me that! He is a storyteller! His words are his truth – just as yours are! Why should you suddenly doubt him, you who dwell in and out of legend?'

This was a different Bella. In the time I had known her she had been first watchful, then quietly encouraging, but this forceful, confident, challenging woman was something I had not seen before. I asked her:

'And you, Bella, where do you dwell?'

She said simply:

'In the Crone.'

And at that her transformation was complete. Her voice and bearing and authority were those of the Old One, but made young again. She said:

'We have conspired to guide you in swanflight to Rab, and to the Rock that ice and sea could not overwhelm where your truth was incarcerated. It is easier in our mountain valleys to adhere to principles of wildness, for nature imposes them as a regime. But in a place like the Rock and the Carse it is not so. What you have done, Tall One, is to leave them thinking that perhaps it should be otherwise.'

'And there is a swan-poet – Rab! – in their midst!'

'You have touched others, Rab among them, but he has none of your certainty and he is distrustful of his swan-art. He is rooted in his Rock and draws his certainty there. But he is wrong to distrust. There is forgiveness in the ways of swans. The forgiveness of nature is at the heart of all wildness, wherever it thrives. Perhaps he will see that in time, although the rootedness of his Rock is a tenacious force.

'There are forces beyond the ways of swans, and there is only the benevolence of time to set against them. I could not counter the Rock-force, so I waited. The years were of little account in the face of eternal renewal. There will always be time enough and certainty enough as long as there are wild swans in the Northlands.

'Rab will be gratified that in your story you chose a new swan from the Carse. There has been none from beyond the mountains since Rolf.'

Rolf! Another crossroads. I said:

'But Rolf lived. My Carse-swan is an invention. I cannot reinvent a life in a story.'

'The life is reinvented in the storyteller, not the story,' said Bella. 'Just as I dwell in the Crone, and she in me, know now that so you dwell in Rolf, and he in you.'

I remembered then the Crone's words:

'With a great poet, what does a death matter?'

My mind flustered. All I could think of was:

'But he was a Lowlander!'

'And you are of the mountains, so you will enrich and purify his work and take it beyond, for you will weld his wisdom to your birthright and the benevolence of swans. To all this, now, you have added a new, a great truth.'

'But how could I travel so far in ignorance?'

'That is of no account, Tall One. What matters is how far you travel in enlightenment.'

It is said in the Northlands, in mountain valleys such as mine, that a single lineage of swans adheres in a few rare instances, to a single watersheet; that when one of the adult birds dies, it will be replaced by one of its own offspring which has matured nearby and remains, waiting, growing older and wiser in a state of readiness to perpetuate the line. The oldest known version of the story says that where the adults are successful and long-lived, the pool of wisdom and readiness among the waiting swans grows beyond the safekeeping of a single nearby watersheet and so must travel. The travelling swans will dispense not just their wisdom but also their native characteristics. Sometimes, two far-travelled swans from different nursery waters will alight on the same still pool and there will be a distilling of rare knowledge.

We lit a fire on that loch shore and sat by it far into the night. A silence of many years lay between us. I stared up at the black bulk of the Mountain of Light. Somewhere in the darkest throes of night, Bella left me. She walked wordlessly to the water, then on into the black depths of the loch. A swan rose from her wake and called once, and flew north on a gentle south wind. But something reached me from the mountain heart, a command borne on a breath of the same wind to keep the mountain's stillness. The fire at my feet did not dowse, but burned untended with a single white flame like the raised wing of a swan.

I will write it now, all that I have come to understand. It is little enough, perhaps. I will write it finally and truly in the ancient book the Crone gave me. It is leather-bound and locked. She had put a withered kiss on its locked clasp and a key on a silver chain round my neck. She had extracted from me this promise: that I must not open it, neither to read from it nor to write in it until I was sure of my own understanding. I am as sure now, this night under the Mountain of Light, as I will ever be.

The Crone had said this too:

'When you have written all that you have come to understand, return, keeping the book safe, for it is the treasury of all our understanding and is given to few.'

So for the first time in twenty years, the key is off my neck. The key turns. The book opens. The paper is as fresh as the day it was made. What is written there startles. There is no treasury of wisdom reaching back through centuries of swan-poets, which is what I had expected, but only a single short paragraph, the ink as fresh as the paper, as though it had just dried. It startles because the handwriting is so familiar. It is unquestionably my own.

I, SWAN WANDERER AND BARD, emissary of the Northlands and the Tribe of All Swans, defender of Wilderness, seek the shedding of the Mountain of Light on this work, for only by the Light of Wilderness that dwells among Mountains can there be Harmony on the Land, that Harmony craved by All Swans.

These words I speak aloud to the mountain, then I begin to write.

CHAPTER 13

'NATURE'S WAY IS TO BUILD A BRIDGE'

IT IS A TROUBLESOME existence, this shifting between the man's world and the swan's. It should be the same world, the same rocks and woods and waters and fellow-travellers. I know that if I moved between the ways of swan and any other creature in all nature, any at all other than man, there would be only common bonds and tolerances to dwell on.

Yet nature's failure with its man creature is unprecedented, such is the paucity of natural virtues left in man. Perhaps man has already considered that the extinction of nature is within his grasp, forgetting that at his core he is still nature himself, that the extinction of nature would also mean the extinction of himself. Perhaps nature has begun to feel that its own very existence is threatened by its own creature. Survival of the species is at the core of nature, so it will hardly preside over its own extinction.

The extinction of man by nature would be easy, of course, but that is not nature's way. Nature's way is to build a bridge, and the architects of such a bridge are the burdened ones of my own tribe. Given time – and nature works in aeons and whole eras – understanding *must* cross. It must, because nothing else is acceptable in nature's eyes. Strength through balance is the first principle of a sound bridge. So nature chooses swans to be the architect of its bridge, for it judges swans to be its one perfect creation, its most joyous beauty, and so sets swans to counterbalance the ugliness of its most imperfect creation; swans must throw the bridge across the abyss that man alone has learned to cross. In that crossing, man also learned to distance himself from nature, to stand outside his own family.

Beyond the abyss he has made a new world and shut himself in it. He has blinded one eye and turned that blindness on nature. He judges his new world easier to inhabit, but that is only true because he has become what he has become, only because of the self-blinding. Ease has become his sole quest, but he has forgotten what he once knew when he lived hand-in-glove with nature, which is that there is no ease.

Swans know there is no ease, only a season in which vigilance may relax by degrees, and in which they can revitalise to be ready again for that other season which is all vigilance, the counterbalances of the wild year. Still men talk distantly of "the balance of nature" as though they understood that vast equation, yet it is the truest thing there is.

So, it is a long and measured span, this bridge nature must build, one that will reach far beyond man's side of the abyss, this because nothing is more certain than that he will widen and deepen his distance before he takes the first tentative and despairing steps of return, only to discover that the way back is already paved and balanced and strong. By then he will have plundered the depths of the land, even the very mountains, for his fuels and his riches; he will have turned in his desperation to the perilous and grudging bounties of his oldest adversary, the sea; then he will have taken on space itself as he begins to try and put distance even between himself and his mother earth. His quest for ease will have grown more and more strenuous.

There will come a point when it occurs to him that his new world is finite, that he cannot exist outside nature. It is only then that he will realise he is beyond the abyss

Then two things will happen. First he will tear at himself, for there will be nothing left to tear at but himself. At last he will contemplate the realisation that he has added self-slaughter to the self-blinding. He will contemplate too the wreckage of the world he built with his own hands for his own ease and, although he will ask himself why, it will not occur to him at first that it failed him because it failed nature and he had forgotten that he too is nature.

Second, a chosen one will turn his head one day to follow a flight of swans and it will lead him along paths of race memory to a time past when a child could look at a flight of swans and see God smile on the face of his hillside. The swans will lift his blindness from him and he will see the need for the bridge. He will find it already built, find it balanced and strong, and he will begin the long journey back across. He will cross back, because, like nature, he knows the alternative – failure to survive – is not acceptable. He will cling to the one quality in nature he has not lost and will not lose, the will of the species to survive that subjugates the will of the individual. He will recognise then what his ancestors denied for so long, that he *is* nature's creature. Because he will be a chosen one, he will have the power to persuade others to follow his example. These few pioneers, explorers of their own errant footsteps, will follow the old trail of their ancestors backwards to where an old misguided beginning almost tore the earth apart. And a great healing will have begun.

Survival is the prime mission of all nature, for what is survival but life itself? And what is life but that elusive harmony that is All Nature, the balance of natural forces.

So man is the imbalance in the equation. Such an imbalance is against the interests of All Nature, so swans have been burdened with a second mission, which is to restore the balance. The bridge is the means of the restoration.

All this I have guessed and learned and understood. But nature does not take you aside one day, clasp your shoulder fraternally and explain the meaning of life in a five-minute lecture for that convinces no-one. Conviction cannot be inherited. It comes from within. That is why I have been twenty years on the mountain road, and why only now do I think I see the purpose of the journey. To think it began by questioning my status as a poet. *Status!* It is of less account than a leaf in an autumn gale. The leaf has at least served a purpose, a pure and faultless purpose.

The mountains soon pared away the layers of my conceit! They merely confronted me with their own great and simple truths.

Great.

Simple.

How overworked and undervalued these two words have become! You learn that too in the mountains where greatness and simplicity are imposed upon you all day, every day. It is one thing to live among such things as I did in the first forty years of my life, with always the chrysalis of the village to limit and inhibit growth. But to shed the chrysalis and go butterfly-bold into the mountain world – that is to be reborn!

Think of it – think of a butterfly that breezes by you in a mountain bog or an alpine meadow or a high forest clearing. You see that brave waved flag of nature and you are briefly gladdened by its tremulous poise, by its beauty. But surely it is not there merely to be beautifully poised? It is there to be!

Now…in your mind's eye, pull back from the butterfly a hundred yards. See how it dwindles while the mountain world enlarges.

Again…in your mind's eye, climb the mountain so that you look down on the meadow. You do not see the butterfly of course and the meadow is no more conspicuous than a patch of lichen. Yet you know the butterfly is there, less than a pinprick on the skin of the mountain world. You know how arduous that world is, even for a man to traverse. Consider a butterfly of all flimsy things in such a setting, subject to the ferocious whim of mountain weather… that a butterfly should choose such a landscape! Why should nature insist on such a perversity?

Still more baffling…the butterfly moves from one alpine meadow to another the only way it can, by crossing the high passes. What journeys! In twenty years, I have done nothing to compare with them. Yet once I had adapted to the spirit of the journey (its purpose would evolve, as you now know), I followed that astounding example, walked butterfly-bold into every mountain wind.

Example. That is why nature puts the butterfly on the mountain, a persevering mote of life-dust to show what is possible amid the great simplicity of the mountain world. Persevere likewise and thrive.

So the first thing I have learned in the mountains is to keep their company not as a man but as nature. The mountains are nature's heartland. All life is cradled here where all great waters spring, and purity is a reservoir of water, rock, light, life. For many centuries, men were moved to place their gods here, and journeyed among mountains fearfully or in the humility of pilgrimage. How that has changed! Men have made a game of the mountain summits. They talk of "conquering" a mountain by reaching its summit. But all they have conquered is their old tribal fear and humility. (I hear my own words back in my own village inn...*it does not do to be small in their company, not insignificant, not humble...*the words of a man, not of nature. How they haunt me!)

How can a mountain be conquered just by putting a foot on its summit? Has it been made lower? Reduced in stature? Has it been made less mountain? Less nature? Has man made it conform to his wishes? No. He has not conquered the mountain in any sense, merely stained it. He no longer cares, as he once did when he went among mountains in the spirit of pilgrimage, that he leaves disfiguring evidence of his passing.

His life is so empty that he will sacrifice it for a summit, disregarding the total mountain. Of course there were deaths among mountain pilgrims, but death on a pilgrimage has virtue, for the pilgrim's quest is for understanding, for a greater closeness with the mountain world, for a glimpse of the Grace of the Mountain.

Someday soon man will climb to the summits of the very highest mountains. It is not beyond him – it has never been beyond him, only beyond his daring. But now that he has made a playing field of the domain of his old gods, nothing is beyond his daring. The climbing of the highest of all the world's mountains, Chomolungma, Goddess Mother of the Wind, will obsess men forever, I fear, but it will remain less of an achievement than the mountain butterfly's brief summer. Look at how man climbs. There is nothing of nature in the climbing. Rather, he climbs to a strategy, as if it were a battle – man *against* the mountain...he uses the very words.

But perhaps he must go through such a phase to win back the old adherence to the spirit of the mountains, so that he can go again as nature. If there is virtue in all this, perhaps it is that when he has reached the summits of all the great mountains of the world (and he will, now that he has the daring), there will emerge one mountaineer great enough to go alone. Going alone, he will see mountains differently from other men and so glean the first glints of a new understanding. He will learn by the particular nature of his efforts to go into the mountains seeking not the summits but understanding of the greatness and the simplicity of mountains. Not man against the mountain but man in harmony with the mountain. Not man climbing as mountaineer, but man climbing as nature, man working with a new awareness of the Grace of the Mountain.

The Grace of the Mountain…how lightly I answered Sammy when he asked me about it. I said…*I see the landscape as the wild swan sees it, from within. You learn the trick of it when you are a wanderer for a living.*

The trick! Did I say that? The only trick I pulled off was to survive my enslavement to that obsessive idea. The quest for the Grace of the Mountain was my obsession and my trial. Now, I am more at ease with the idea, thanks to the perceptions of nature as wild swan. Yet, for the same reason, I have been burdened with a knowledge, and that being-at-ease is forever tempered with the burden. All nature learns to live with the burden. Even the mountain butterfly shoulders it portion, while man has learned to live ignorantly and unburdened.

The last words the Crone said to me as her brittle mouth kissed the ancient book were these:

'The Grace of the Mountain go with you, Tall One.'

Knowing what she knew then, she passed on to me the blessing and the burden of our troubled tribe in those words. She had also echoed the stranger in the village inn who had in turn invoked Rolf. All this I slung on my shoulder with my pack the day I took to the pilgrim road. At first I bore the words bravely before me, like a crusader's banner. I relished their sound on my tongue and spun them often out into the mountain air as a password and greeting to the mountain spirits. I watched them form in my mind. Day after day as I wandered into ever-wilder mountain lands, I gathered eagerly fragments (as I thought) of the Grace of the Mountain, arranging them into a kind of anthology of wilderness. It seemed at first as if merely being there was enough, the pilgrimage an end in itself, that the Grace of the Mountain would fall within my grasp by the very fact of the pilgrimage.

Had I known then how far I would have to travel to reach this point, would I have ever set off? I wonder.

At first the pilgrimage was a liberation. I was inspired by the early journeys. Poems came away in fistfuls, like berries, and whenever I met other wilderness dwellers, they marvelled at the nature of my journey and cheered me on with many forms of encouragement.

An old hermit put a stop to that. He greeted me briefly. He smiled wordlessly at my stories and poems, listened attentively (still wordlessly) to my raw philosophies, fed and watered me hospitably. But as I prepared to leave and thanked him, he spoke for the first time since his few words of greeting. What he said was this:

'I have enjoyed this. I am sorry. I converse poorly. In my long solitude I have lost the art. You converse so beautifully.'

He paused, his face a mask of troubles, seeking out the forgotten means of expression. Then he went on:

'But I wonder…are you sure…sure that you have found it…found the Grace of the Mountain…the true grace…for I worry…worry that it seems to have been so lightly won? It is such a crucial journey that you make. For all our sakes…I beg you…look again, will you…to be sure…to be sure of the grace. I wish you a fair and a following wind, pilgrim.'

A few dozen words, all that he spoke while I must have spoken many thousands through the two days and nights I was with him, yet he had spoken enough to unravel my first three years in the wilderness. He had breached a dam that had held in check the floodwaters of doubt. Then I almost drowned in questions. I made a vow: no more hermits, villagers, hospitality. Seek out ever deeper wilderness, seek out truth, seek out the grace, the true grace. Then the dark days began.

I would waken at 3am to find my mind dismantling the very words of the phrase...the...Grace...of...the...Mountain...until I had corrupted even the very simplicity of the idea. I would worry for a week at a time about that first 'the'. Did the Crone imply when she said '*the* Grace of the Mountain go with you' that there were many graces and that I must seek out the one true grace? In which case, were the others deceptions or merely lesser graces? What a torment would begin to rage within me then, a torment fuelled by obsession and solitude. Each word was dissected thus as my mind plumbed the labyrinths of the quest. The prize I craved was a single pure thread of understanding, a shining truth, but only darker and darker depths claimed me. Rock and ice walls hemmed me in, high passes led only to new hemming walls. In the few moments, snatches of stillness, when the obsession relinquished its hold, I would come upon myself sitting alone by a glacier perhaps, a scrap of corrupted, purposeless life, so much less than the butterfly, and I could see and fear the madness within me. What road was this for a poet? What fate for a teller of tales? What had been my dire misdeed that had warranted such a penance?

Well, I would tell myself, as though I addressed that second self I had chanced on, *it has been penance enough now. Return. Go back and live quietly and let your mind heal. None will criticise you for that. Your village kin will hail your return. The Crone will not blame you, for she will see the depths of suffering, the weight of burden.*

Then the obsession was on me again, my mind no longer my own but a fevered explorer, daring amid the ever-darkening ways of the mountain labyrinth.

Seek out ever deeper wilderness.

Seek out truth.

Seek out *the* grace.

Seek...seek...seek...it intoned.

Each day became a ritual, indistinguishable from the next and the last. Each demanded only that it should propel me through more mountain miles. I would walk because I had walked the day before, because I would walk the day after. Snow and storm and heatwave slowed me but never stopped me for long. On, on, on, unguided, propelled forward.

Each night became a ritual: the simplest of food I had gathered or caught, troublesome sleep, troublesome sleeplessness. Nothing could rein in my mind at night, nothing cool its fever, nothing inhibit the darkness and depths where it toiled. By day I could mark off tree after tree, rock after rock, as they slid past me, and mark them as progress, but by night under rock or blanket or star, I was defenceless and the labyrinthine madness was on me again, pitiless as locusts. How I dreaded and loathed the nights, how I yearned for dawns.

Yet it was sleep that guarded the one fragment of dream to which I clung, a barely buoyant lifebelt, a fingernail's hold on a sense of purpose, that only the journey itself had brought into my life. Every night, somewhere among the torments there came a respite, the same brief and unfailing dream, an image far-off and still, of a white flame. That flame, I sensed, symbolised journey, purpose, destiny, life, the reasons to go on. Somehow, through that dream, I never quite stopped believing that one day I would sit and warm myself at that flame and the thing would be done, the single shining silken thread revealed, the Grace of the Mountain acknowledged. In all my life had become, it remained the one good and unwavering presence, a cold heartbeat, an Arctic fire, a single source of purity, unstained. Never did the dream reveal more than that, but nor did it fail to throw its beacon light on the journey. I began at last to pray to that dream for it finally became all in my world that I could trust. By then I had even come to doubt the mountains themselves, as if they too were somehow part of a colossal conspiracy of madness.

So I walked through the years, until at last I crossed one more watershed and looked down into a broader valley than I had ever known. At first glance, the breadth and brightness of the valley and the total absence of mountains beyond so startled me that I recoiled from it. I distrusted its gold and green show and turned back, back into the mountains, back to the safe familiarity of the dark torment, reclaimed by the labyrinth. At once a great weariness overwhelmed me. It had been a hard pass to climb, and my mind was duller than I had ever known. I chose to spend the night on the crest of the pass. The morning, or the morning after that, would be time enough for the valley. That night, of all nights, there was no dream. The dream failed me.

I rose in the dawn, sleepless and weary beyond anything I could remember, feeling old and stiff and sore. One thought now possessed my mind, obliterating every other sensibility. It was to put an end to the journey, to the torment of life itself. Without the life-fire of the dream, the flame of survival had been snuffed out. Nature's purpose was finally defeated, and without that, what right had I to live? What point in life?

Far below on the floor of the bright valley lay a small lake, smooth as uncreased silk in the early morning. I resolved to crease that silk with my drowning.

It took three hours to reach the lake by which time the sun had stitched gold and silver into the silken gray. At the water's edge I threw off my ragged clothes knowing I would have no more use for them. I was utterly calm when, without pause or uncertainty, I walked into the water. Its chill barely touched me and I was quickly in the lake's depths, muffling sound, dulling light, sinking down.

'Now drown.'

I rose towards the light, stood on the surface of the water and threw a wide arc of swan's wings at the sun, each wing a cool, white Arctic flame. I had become my own dream.

The Grace of the Mountain is the perfection of nature, the one pure source.

Its symbol is the wild swan that hatches on a quiet water in the shadow of the mountain, and through that swan, the tribe of all swans. Through swans, nature insinuates its perfection, its truth, across the earth, even into the midst of men. In his towns man finds swans. These are a bond between him and natural beauty. These confide in him, but he sees that other swans are wild and aloof and unconfiding. The swans that confide in him remind him of his own lost wildness.

My journey had retraced his steps across the abyss that guards all nature's realm. It had become necessary for one man to cross back so that a pilgrim route could begin. I have become, through my crossing, a single plank in that long, slow bridge which in time all humanity must cross.

The Crone had said:

'Absorb all that the mountains will give you, then stand for a winter beyond the furthest edge of the mountains. See them with the eyes of those who live beyond.'

So I came to the Rock, to the Place of Strifes, and what I have left behind is the raw material from which a new plank can be fashioned, a second plank on a long, slow bridge.

I looked up from my writing to the Mountain of Light across the loch, sought its blessing on what I had written. I turned the key in the book's clasp and kissed it.

Somewhere in the northern night, Bella would be waiting for me. I rose and stepped once more into the waters, the kindly darkening waters of swans.

CHAPTER 14

SAMMY'S STORY – THE MOUNTAIN OF LIGHT

১৯৩৯

SAMMY, THE ONE they called "Futret", the weasel-headed, weasel-curious Sammy, Sammy the thinker, gathered up fistfuls of papers. They were coarse scraps and did not stack evenly. He had never been given to writing before, and only a writer's house is well stocked with reams of clean writing paper that stack evenly when you gather them up. But Sammy had found paper. Some of it was brown wrapping paper cut into rough rectangles. Some of it was the backs of old bills, and some the blank pages torn from the end of a few old books, and an old envelope made four sheets once he'd torn it carefully, for the address had never been written nor the stamp stuck. A tiny, weasel-footed handwriting explored every bare half-inch of paper. He numbered the sheets carefully, following a bizarre system of arrows that sometimes led from the foot of the page to a sideways exploration of the margins, to the other side of the paper, and from there to a last unexplored corner of the first side.

Ever since the Wanderer had gone, the thing had consumed him. It was as if a sown seed had found nourishment in his thin head, and demanded root and stem and leaf and flower. That singular mountain shape on his skyline, Ben Ledi, the Mountain of Light, that was the shape of the seed. It had been there on his workaday skyline all his life, of course, but now its image lodged in his head like a starry saxifrage in a rock crevice, and he would see it in daydreams and sleeping dreams, in the clouds and in the fire. Day after day he walked out to the knoll below the castle, a north-facing outcrop of the Rock, to where he could watch the mountain catch the light and haul down the passing spring snow. He saw it gather the summer-green folds of its brightest garb, saw these grow dull as the summer grew heavy and old and the heather splashed the slopes with its uncanny, un-Scottish-looking purple.

He saw the September sun sharpen and gild the mountain. In October it whitened again. It was a year since the Wanderer had arrived. Sammy thought about the impact of that old October on his life. He re-checked the order of the papers. He was nervous. Tonight, he would read his story to his four friends round the fire in the back bar of the Castle Inn, where it had all begun for them.

Or had it? Sammy wondered about Rab, who had changed since the Wanderer left. Where had it all begun for Rab? How far back? He shrugged.

He saw himself in his living room mirror. He tried a dress rehearsal, reading the thing aloud to his own reflection.

It was fine on the page, he thought, but getting it off the page was so bloody difficult. That was why he was nervous. So this is the story he read out to the weasel face in the glass, the story he would tell to his friends an hour or two later, the story he called *The Mountain of Light.*

Back in the town, they said the mountain's heart was a light.

They said the mountain hid its heart behind a curtain of rock that fell a thousand feet to the smashed mountain wall that was now a boulderfield.

They said the light was the one thing – the only pure thing – that was left in the land because it had never cast a human shadow, and it had never lit a human face. And it never would.

The town was twenty miles away from the mountain across the wide Carse of farms and two rivers that joined near the town and went round it like a slow snake. The town had grown down from a castle on a great Rock, the Rock that was an old volcano, a throwback. The gray town seeped down the skirts of the Rock. It was like a stain the way it seeped out onto the low ground of the Carse. Its name was once famous all over Europe, for kings (and once a queen) and their armies had prized it, and fought for it. Not now. Now it was a quiet place.

Now the loudest skirmishes were among the haggling farmers at the markets, and the Saturday night drinkers in a certain back bar at the inn high on the Rock, hard under the castle, the castle that sometimes girned at you on black rainy nights, or reared above you like a black stallion ready to bring its hooves down on your head when the wind blew hard. And sometimes it was just good to have its strength there whenever you crossed your own threshold and looked up.

Pilgrims rested in its shadow before journeying on to the mountain. They believed in the legend of the light, because of the first long-haired, leathery-faced, mountain-thirled pilgrim of all who stayed a winter in the town but couldn't take his mind or his eyes off the mountain. A few friends that lived in the oldest and darkest shadow of the castle had listened to him and cracked with him all through that winter and gossip about him had spread all across the town, and that put a new legend on that Rock that fairly bulged at the seams already with old ones. The legend spread far afield. Then the pilgrims started coming.

The mountain is clearly seen from the oldest part of the town. But it's more than that. It's like a presence, a bit like the castle, except that whiles it's distant and whiles it's too near for comfort, or so it seems if you watch it long enough and often enough. Between the foot of the Rock and the foothills of the Highlands where the mountain rises...there lies the Carse that ebbs and flows, a sea of corn, from one to the other in restless summer winds.

[At this the listeners would sit forward, exchanging glances, marking a sudden change in the style and the bearing of the story-teller, as though some presence was in *him*. They saw and heard the Wanderer in Sammy, "the wren become eagle" as Walter would remark later.]

So the pilgrims gathered in the lee of the castle and filled the town's inns and hotels and other lodgings, paused for a night of rest (many had travelled far already), savouring the mountain at arm's length before testing its embrace. Then they would begin to walk out from the town in the early morning while the fields still wore their smoored gray, while the foxes and owls still prospected among the farms, the badgers among the woods, while the wild swans still sat folded and at ease on their waters.

Mist still clung low to the river and in high shrouds it lay about the shoulders and waist of the Mountain of Light.

That was the quiet world the pilgrims stepped into, following a beaten trail among the fields, climbing among the foothills, pausing at the end of their day's march at the foot of the mountain to honour it, such was the strength of the legend that had begun with the Wanderer, so many years ago now. Many of the pilgrims had this in common – that they had begun to place their gods in the mountains again, and nature was at the centre of many a new religion. There were none of the extravagances that bedevilled the old religions and corrupted old churches and governments. It had not been a fast transition but had seeped glacier-slow down from the Northlands of the world, where, the legend said, the Wanderer still lived, half-poet, half-swan, maybe half some kind of god or other. At last the change reached the mountain edge above the Carse and the long memories of the Rock folk began to tell the first pilgrims about the Wanderer.

The place suddenly became suffused with the new adherence to nature's way, and the Rock and the mountain became a focal point, and the old town's name was once again on the lips of half of Europe, but this time as a shrine. Somehow, in the midst of all that zeal, the legend of the light was born. What we know of the legend from the accounts of many pilgrims is this:

There is a certain rock high on the summit ridge of the Mountain of Light which is holed clean through, a pierced slab. At a certain hour on the longest day of the year (and if it is a good day, for clouds cling amorously to the mountain for days at a time), a beam of sunlight falls through the hole into a high meadow. Men saw that beam (which men and where remains a mystery for they came and went five thousand years ago) and because they lived in primitive awe of nature, they ritualised it as something sacred. It is likely that they were sun-worshippers (in which case they must have found the mountain weather a sore disappointment), and saw in the holed rock and its sunshaft a direct path of communication to their sun-god. Their sun-worship might have been nothing more than the worship of a god who can be seen, an omnipresent symbol of a deity that suited their nomadic ways.

They paused at the Mountain of Light long enough to build a phenomenon, a monument of such ingenuity that its purpose and the method of its construction have baffled every succeeding age of enlightenment and otherwise. It is a stone circle, but where would such stones have come from, for their nearest surviving kin are deep in the Arctic lands? The irresistible conclusion is that they brought the rocks with them, yet each one weighs many tons and there are forty-three of them! The mystery has exercised great minds and small for millennia. One expert mind has asked:

Did they bring the rocks seeking a situation to erect a preconceived monument (a sun temple with a blueprint!), or, having stumbled on the midsummer moment of the sun and the holed slab, did they judge it a significant enough occurrence to send squads of fetchers and carriers back to their mysterious heartlands for the raw materials they were accustomed to work with, their own native rocks?

To which a second expert mind countered:

If they arrived five thousand years ago, surely they would have come from the south, creeping up Europe's Atlantic coast? No-one came wandering these seas from the north, not then.

Ah, said a third, but these were the swan-folk, who have been in the Northlands longer than the ice! But the academics scoffed at that and bent their minds to the puzzle again, yet to no avail, for puzzle it remains, the evidence as spectacular as it is baffling.

Forty stones stand in a ring, some twice the height of a man, some thrice, some flat-topped, some pointed, some rounded. One of them is holed and faces the mountain. The shape of the hole matches perfectly the shape of the hole in the mountain summit rock, but is perhaps one tenth of its size. This too has baffled the great minds who have climbed and wondered and measured and marvelled at the perfect reduction of the man-made hole. They ask themselves:

It is one thing to make a mathematically correct miniature copy of the summit hole, but how would the builders have gauged that the granite hole at three thousand feet would weather in precisely the same way as their sandstone replica fifteen hundred feet lower, so that no matter how long the two stood to be compared, they would evolve perfectly in proportion?

At the centre of the circle are three more stones, two tall and slim and close, the third a recumbent slab with a small depression in the top like a font. All this is so arranged that when the sun passes through the mountain rock hole at midsummer, it also passes through the replica in the stone circle and alights on the water that inevitably lies in the font (for it has never been known to dry out, and that too is unexplained). What manner of faith was at work that it inspired such a labour to harness a sunbeam to a puddle?

So the pilgrims who crossed from the town on its Rock to the sunbeam on its mountain rock had much to preoccupy them as they walked, as they watched the Mountain of Light separate itself from the skyline and stand forward while the other mountains receded. They would see as they began the climb out of the Carse how the mountain ruled that landscape of the Highland Edge, how it must have preyed on the minds of the Carse folk in their farms. There would surely never be any getting used to it...either it was there before them shutting out a great pyramid-wedge of the sky, or it was behind them, a vast, dark crouch.

You can imagine that the thin file of pilgrims thickened towards midsummer to throng and jockey among the standing stones and catch that five thousand-year-old trick of light, and some said too many came then, either for the good of the mountain or the pilgrimage. But others, a more stoical tribe, came in the autumn and the winter when the sun put down well to the south and there was no sorcery in the rocks. They had little enough time for imagery and the formality of the stone circle, and as for its great age, what was that but a blink compared to the age of the mountain itself? And wasn't it just as man-made in its way as all the other artefacts of all the other religions that followed the sun-worshippers? They argued instead that it was the light at the heart of the

Mountain of Light that set it apart as holy ground, for it was pure nature. It was, they said, a flame, a timeless survivor of those fires that had lit the earth's first darkness and lit it still, a single white flame, they said, as pure as a swan's wing. The light could not be seen, not by men at least, but the sense of it could be achieved and was most vivid when the land was darkest, and that was midwinter.

It seems to me that those were the true pilgrims, for their truth was pared away to essential simplicities. These winter pilgrims would tell you that the stone circle builders recognised the truth of the mountain, and that their sun monument was a symbolic rendering of the light down to the level of ordinary mortals; yet surely they had tried to harness the light, that still white flame that was perfect nature, for their own religious ends, and in trying to harness it they had sullied it, or at least the sense of it. Their faith in the existence of the still white flame was not enough, and they had to resort to this trickery to convince their fellows. So you see that even among the pilgrims of the new nature creed there was strife to be found here. Oh, this town, and its wearisome way with strifes!

Then there came the obsessed, the men not of nature but of science, for whom the idea of a blind faith in the light was just fuel for their donnish jokes. They confronted the Mountain of Light with their new sciences and a great deal of sophisticated equipment, and they pronounced the stone circle a Victorian fake and scorned the very existence of a light at the heart of the mountain because their science was infallible and their science could not detect it. There was no light. It was a myth after all, and probably the mysterious man called the Wanderer had begun it all.

That fanned a great controversy and suddenly the Place of Strifes grew clamorous again, the stage on which one more strife disported. More scientists came, academics gorged themselves with new theories, journalists offered them all to the wider world. The pilgrim business boomed. Innkeepers and publicans mopped their brows from dawn till dawn and sang in tune with their tills. The townsfolk began to invent and rehearse carefully worded snatches of "folk wisdom" knowing that at any moment they would be confronted by the throng of journalists and asked to pass a judgment on the latest theory, the newest twist. For example, a shoemaker would shake his head fretfully and say:

'It is a brave but a foolish man who holds a candle to the Mountain of Light.' It was meaningless gibberish and he walked away grinning, but for the next week or two, no pilgrim would set out for the mountain unless he was shod by *that* shoemaker.

Then came the unscrupulous, the money-makers, waving chequebooks at the town council, sums undreamed of. The townsfolk were never the kind to be impressed by fool's gold and habitually held such people to ridicule, but this...

'This will make the town immortal,' said one town official who was quite seduced by the smell of so much money, and there were many who danced to the same tune, such were the sums involved. Others in the town said no, the Rock had already made the town immortal, and some time ago at that, but the money men prevailed. Certain influential heads were turned by entrepreneurs promising a new "pilgrim experience", and they were permitted to build the most monstrous thing on the Gowan Hill below the castle that looks north-west to the Mountain of Light. What it was they built was a replica, a huge scale model of the mountain and its stone circle, and using lasers and all kinds of trickery, they showed how the sun worked the sorcery of the two holed rocks, only they could make it happen every day of the year.

But it was worse than that. The inside of the model was like an old round theatre with one vast glass wall that faced the real Mountain of Light, and in the centre of the sunken stage, surrounded by seats for three-quarters of the circle, there was a single white flame (fed by gas) and that was supposed to be the light that no-one had ever seen.

Now, bellowed the money men, you can *see* the light that could never be seen, and be purified by it, and of course there was a price to be paid to see the flame and watch the distant mountain through a false mountainside of glass. Now there was no need for the pilgrimage!

The queues lengthened and the prices rose and the town on the Rock fairly boomed while the Pilgrim Road between the town and the mountain was silent and grew green again. But then an undercurrent of dissent was in the air among some of the townsfolk. This, they said, is not our way. They had always been accustomed to visitors to the castle and the other old stone souvenirs of the town's story and strifes, but this was different. They never had their own town to themselves now from one year's end to the next, and the streets filled with the stench of corruptions. They felt betrayed.

The Gowan Hill below the castle, which had been the most corrupted thing of all, that was theirs, their land by ancient right, and whether or not they believed in the legend of the light, they raged at this reducing of the mountain to a cheap trick, a mockery. Whereas they had always had time for the first pilgrims and the stories they brought with them into their old inns, they disliked the new legions of gawpers who wanted the Rock and the castle and the town and the mountain and the legend of the light all wrapped into a single package to consume in an hour and quite without effort. In a random way, the dissent of the townspeople began to find a voice.

So there was a night when a small knot of old cronies took their familiar places by the fire in a certain old back bar in the town, turning their faces to the fire, the arc of their backs to the loud throng of visitors. As they bent their heads close and lowered their voices and some of the visitors proclaimed their surliness in loud voices and complained how they shut out the fire to everybody else, their brows furrowed, and their fingers stabbed the old wooden table in the heightened passion of their conversation. Occasionally one of their number would push aside a chair and weave through the throng to refill a fistful of glasses, and a more perceptive stranger would notice that the drinks were bought by each man in turn, a sun-wise progress round the table. The barman would explain to anyone who asked that these were guardians of an old tradition, and there were plenty in the town who sympathised with them, but who could stand in the path of progress, eh?

They were old men themselves, and some said their fathers or their grandfathers or their grandfathers' fathers – who knew any more? – had sat round the same fire with the first pilgrim of all and learned from him the mysterious and troubling swan-stories of the Northlands, and maybe the true nature of the legend of the light – who knew? The secrecy in which these men now shrouded the guardianship of their knowledge was unbreachable, not by reporters, moneymen, pliers of drink, breachable by nothing and no-one. That night, it was not stories they told nor ancient mysteries they discussed, nor had it been that way for many nights. They were plotting, nothing less than the slaying of the monster in their midst, that and finding a way back to the simpler relationship between town and mountain that had prevailed for so long.

At the centre of the group was a man whose age was hard to fathom. If anything, he looked younger than the others – sixty perhaps – but ageless about the eyes and capable of apparently recalling events far in the town's past with the kind of detail of one who had lived through such moments. He was Rab, and some said there had been a Rab among the first group of cronies, the ones that knew the Wanderer that started it all, and that this was the same Rab, grown only as old as those who know eternal renewal ever grow. Such a story was unlikely to win you many adherents in such a Rock-rooted place, and if you were foolish enough to broach the subject with Rab himself he could put a look on you to turn you to stone.

This Rab now spoke:

'I have heard,' he began, and that the other graying heads leaned closer. Rab had antennae that "heard" things beyond the scope of the others, and they had long since learned the folly of questioning his sources. In any case, as their natural and unelected leader he had never failed them, and nor had his information. Their loyalty was just as unquestioning. He seemed to them at times to be hewn from the very Castle Rock, such was his rootedness in the place, such his knowledge of it, his awareness of its timelessness that seemed to attend him like a shadow when he moved through its old streets. You could only achieve such a thing by growing very old and remaining as unaged as the Rock, and it was that which his bar-room cronies acknowledged and deferred to and loved.

Others who knew him less thoroughly distrusted his feyness, found him a troubling presence. Yet he rarely spoke outwith that back-turned arc of men at the fire, except to order his share of drinks according to that strict sun-wise ritual. If you met his gaze you shrank from his eyes, for they looked not at you but far, far through you, as if focused on something a great distance behind where you stood. Then suddenly you would find him smiling at you, such a smile you felt blessed by it, and then his back was to you and he was crossing wordlessly to the fire, and you did not know whether to love the man or despise him, he left you feeling so helpless.

So the loyalty within the bar-room arc tarred them all with the same fey-shaded brush and isolated their coterie within their own community, although the same townsfolk who held them at arms' length would rouse to their defence against the loud ridicule of the milling tides of tourists, who queued to see the fake mountain and its fake flame and turned indifferent backs on nature's mountain.

'I have heard,' Rab was saying, 'of a swan skin high on the mountain.'

His friends were at once intrigued and uneasy, as they always were at talk of swans given the role they had played in the town's story since their forefathers admitted the Wanderer to their hearth. Mostly they had understood it no more than their descendants did now, and now there was a swan skin high on the Mountain of Light, on the shore of a small high lochan called Lochan nan Corp in the old Gaelic tongue that named the landscape, meaning the Small Loch of the Corpse.

Around the inn fire they waited in a new silence for Rab to go on but his head was bowed and his brow was black, and still they waited, each one nurturing the same unspoken question and wondering inside themselves at the nature of the burden that bowed him. Then Rab resumed in a hoarse whisper:

'I assume it means the Wanderer?'

'You mean he's *back*?'

'I think so.'

A chorus of disbelief…

'Yer crazy Rab.'

'Aye, daft Neebor, nuts.'

'And yet…'

That "and yet…" was from the quiet thinker of the group, a small voice and soft-spoken among the loud incredulity. Rab seized on it as a drowning man on a passing lifebelt.

'And yet…?' he invited the speaker to continue.

'And yet,' the soft voice said, 'he always seemed to be thinking and talking and writing in his own kind of time, as if our kind of time didn't matter. We never learned to think the way he did, you know, so far back or so far ahead. So my grandfather always said. He spoke about him all the time.'

Rab nodded.

'Sammy…aye, they were close, him and the Wanderer. But you said "writing". What do you know of his writing?'

'Sammy had a book,' the soft-voiced one resumed, 'an ancient thing with a lock. He showed me it once. I never forgot it, although I was very young. The Wanderer had written in it, about building a bridge between man and nature, a bridge that spanned centuries, as if he was the architect of such a bridge.'

'What happened to the book?' asked Rab.

'Sammy drowned it. In the lochan on the mountain.'

Groans and gasps around the firelit table. Rab shook his head, then demanded:

'Why have you said nothing about this before?'

'Sammy swore me to secrecy. He was very old and I was very young. He could hardly climb up to the lochan by that time, and died not long afterwards. He was troubled by the burden of the knowledge he had got from the book, and trusted no-one to guard it. So he built a lead box, wrapped the book carefully, locked it and sealed it in the box and carried it up to the lochan, because the Wanderer had thought of it as a sacred place. Sammy told me that day the Wanderer had said to him the lochan had a purity, like a pure white flame which could not be extinguished. So he committed the knowledge of the book to the purity of the lochan-like-a-flame. And what I am saying, I suppose, is that somehow I always assumed the Wanderer or someone like him would find a way of retrieving the book if it was ever needed again. And now you say there is a swan skin by the lochan.'

Another voice asked:

'So what do we do now?'

'We make one last pilgrimage,' said Rab, 'to the lochan.'

'To the Wanderer?'

'To the Wanderer.'

'When do we leave?'

Rab looked round the crowded room, listened to its clamour, its loud and alien voices, remembered how it had once been, the comfort he had drawn here so he felt hewn from the very Rock on which the inn was built. Now he drew nothing from the room, nothing at all, and he knew at last he was done with the place, done with the Rock-hewn life. He stood.

'Now,' he said.

He tipped his chair forward against the table and motioned to the others to do the same, a sun-wise progression round the table.

The five reached the lochan in the early morning having walked through the night and climbed through the dawn. They were cold and tired but the measured step of their progress had not faltered. At the lochan, a tall and larch-straight man rose to greet them. He was broad and weathered and though his body was agile and lean his face looked old, for it wore the whiplashes of many winds. The white unwavering flame of swanflight was in his eyes of glacier-green. He embraced Rab with great warmth. To do so he had first to lay down an ancient book he had been holding, a book with a lock. He had a key on a chain about his neck.

Soon, there were only six dark circles widening on the water, and no sound to challenge the whisper of a soft south wind.

The Castle Inn in Stirling has a strange monument. Before the fire at one end of the old back bar there is a table much older than all the others. Five chairs sit there, each one tipped forward against the table. It is known or made known to all who drink there that the table may not be used. The innkeeper is often asked about it. He will tell you that years ago, five of the establishment's oldest customers walked out and did not return, and that same night a huge scale model of the Mountain of Light, that had stood on the Gowan Hill below the Castle and attracted visitors from all over the world, was destroyed by fire. There were many deaths, for the flames had spread to the roof timbers of the inn which was packed with visitors who treated the artificial mountain almost like a shrine. Many of the townspeople had resented the way the thing mimicked and commercialised nature, and after the fire it was never rebuilt and nature reclaimed the hill, as you can see. The strange thing, the barman will tell you, was that in the ruins of the inn fire, that old wooden table and those five tipped-forward chairs failed to burn, and no-one can explain that.

Back in the town, they said the mountain's heart was a light. They said the mountain hid its heart behind a curtain of rock that fell a thousand feet to the smashed mountain wall that was now a boulderfield. They said the light was the one pure thing left in the land because it had never cast a human shadow nor lit a human face, and never would. And some said no, it was just the low winter sun striking an oblique white light on the still surface of a high lochan where the wild whooper swans sometimes paused.